BOUND BY LAW

MEN OF HONOR

NEW YORK TIMES BESTSELLING AUTHOR

STEPHANIE TYLER

WRITING AS

SE JAKES

MEN OF HONOR, BOOK 2

The one man he can't forget is the one whose memories could destroy them all.

After the one man he trusted disappeared, it took Law Connor ten years to take a chance on another relationship. Trouble is, right about the time he's finally ready to let go of the past, the past stages a hostile takeover.

Back when they were teens, Styx was the boy with no memory. He and Law had each other's backs until he was forced to leave to keep Law safe. Now a CIA agent, he's finally discovered who he is, and why he's a hunted man.

Detective Paulo McMannus has almost succeeded in helping Law forget his lost love when Styx comes plowing back into their lives. No way is Paulo giving up his lover without a fight.

Suddenly Law finds himself on the run with Styx, the man who can still bring him to his knees...and with Paulo, the man who brought him back to life. The worst part? He can't choose between them. And it's getting harder to remember why he should.

Warning: Contains rough language, rougher sex and warriors who fall hard for one another.

For my editor, Jennifer Miller, for helping me to make my stories the best they can be—and for loving these guys as much as I do.

PROLOGUE

He'd been Styx for literally as long as he could remember.

If there was a birth certificate that proved otherwise, he'd yet to stumble on it. His reissued one gave a date of birth that seemed reasonable, since his old hospital records were simply gone—it was as if he'd materialized out of nowhere. Having absolutely no memory of his youth before the age of sixteen didn't help matters any. His first centered on waking up on a bench in Central Park, wandering into a gay club where he ended up crashing on a cot in the back for a while, until the owner invited him home.

The owner was Greg, who'd figured Styx for underage and had given him a refuge and a new life. The one who'd helped him get the new birth certificate and ID. At first, Styx had waited for the catch, assumed Greg wanted something from him. As it turned out, Greg did. He wanted Styx to grow up safe and sound, was paying it forward, the way a man had done for him years earlier.

Law had already been there about two years when Greg took Damon in, followed in swift succession by Styx.

None of them were formally adopted by any means—CPS wouldn't have looked kindly on a forty-year-old gay man taking in underage gay boys, but it had been aboveboard from the start, a light in all three men's lives that ultimately saved them—from outside forces as well as themselves. It had been a real home—and Styx owed the man everything.

All three had been straddling the line between boy and man and had been drawn to Greg as if he were some sort of Guardian Angel. Styx had never changed his opinion of that.

Greg had never asked for a penny. He'd died about sixteen years ago and Styx still missed the hell out of him. Missed the other men as well. Styx had left them when he was almost twenty without so much as a note in the middle of the night when a threat from his past came out of the blue, and he turned himself in to the CIA a year later, when the burden of his past got too much to bear alone. For the past sixteen years, he'd lived like the spook he was.

He'd kept up with Law and Damon—both had gone the way of the military, and they remained friends, running clubs together up until a few months ago. He'd only allowed himself to visit Law three times, and although he'd never come right out and told Law or Damon what he was, both men had spent enough time around elite forces to be able to sniff out the fact that he was a spook.

It was what he did—who he was. And lately, it had him missing Law, the love of his damned life and the man he left behind, to the point where he was driving himself crazy.

But the past…it was coming for him again. Although he knew why, he still had yet to remember it for himself. And now, he had a chance to find out the full, fleshed-out version, and he was driving to reach the place where it would be delivered to him.

And so Styx walked up the stairs and closed the door, and he waited for the knock that would change his life.

LC slammed out of Crave, the BDSM club he used to be part owner of and where he never should've gone back to in the first place, got into his Porsche, and let it coast along the deserted streets. He willed himself to relax, let the music pound through him, but he knew that wouldn't work.

No, he needed to fuck. He'd already fought, slamming the shit out of some asshole who'd tried to throw his weight around at the club. And LC, already primed for action, had taken over, ignoring Damon telling him to stand down.

Damon, his friend and other former owner of the club, had yanked him off the man and hadn't said another word, and LC had left before he did or said something he'd regret.

He was so damned tired of regrets. Tired of being alone and thrashing around at night, dreaming of two different men—one he loved and one he was falling for.

Thing was, the past few weeks, the dreams had been…

different. And it was time to start listening to where his subconscious was pushing him.

The houses flew by him and he knew where he had to go, the destination calling him like a beacon.

He headed up the walk and let himself in the main door, a skill he'd used widely and well for years, almost long forgotten, and it made him smile when he remembered it easily. The lock clicked open and he went up the three flights with stealth and thought about doing the same to the apartment door.

But he knocked instead, two hard bangs, and he heard movement inside. He hoped the man was alone, wanted him to be—needed him to be, even though he had no right to ask or expect that at all.

Where the hell have you been? was written all over his face, and the man refused to let LC in at first. But LC persisted and Paulo relented, and finally LC barreled in, grabbing and kissing the man until he stopped resisting and twined his hands in LC's hair and moaned into his mouth.

He practically carried the man back inside the apartment, kicked the door closed behind him before they tumbled to the floor, clothes ripping off, grunting, grabbing.

Then he pulled back. "I've been thinking about you. Dreaming about you…can't stop."

"About time," was all the other man said before LC covered his mouth again with a kiss.

The knock startled him, although it shouldn't have. Styx hesitated before opening the door—a highly trained, gun-carrying, wet-work assassin hesitated opening the damn door to his own apartment and yeah, maybe it was time to think about getting the hell out of Dodge.

But he opened it, the door to his past, took the envelope from the man's hands and didn't look him in the eye. His hands shook, making the fat envelope flutter in his fingers, the only sound in the otherwise silent room.

The world was silent at three in the morning, and typically, he liked that. Now, he longed for sounds, any sound but the tearing of the envelope and the unraveling of a life long buried by necessity.

He held that life in his hands, and the responsibility, the revelations, all threatened to crush him if he wasn't careful.

For the first time in a long time he realized he no longer wanted to be careful.

1

Paulo wasn't taking no for an answer, so LC had no choice but to concede to having dinner with the man. They were getting past the anonymous fucking stage and Paulo knew that, took advantage of him when he was weak from orgasms. Hence, the fancy goddamned dinner at an expensive restaurant where the detective obviously knew the staff. They got a private table in the back and appetizers began arriving without them having to place any orders. Paulo kept pouring the wine and LC got looser with each glass, and he knew he'd be going home with Paulo again that night for sure. Or maybe he'd take Paulo back to his new apartment for the first time, a new place, a fresh start…the same guy more than once, and that was a fucking record that had remained unbroken for ten years.

"Tell me what LC stands for," Paulo murmured now. "Or I'll tie you down and fuck it out of you."

"That's incentive to tell you?" LC asked as he scanned his menu for the main courses, not wanting to let Paulo see how turned on he got when Paulo spoke like that. Because he did so easily, his eyes hot, and LC remembered how good his body had felt against the younger man's.

Before last night, it had been about three months since he'd seen him last. Paulo had come to visit LC in the hospital after he'd thwarted an attacker who'd been hurting men outside Crave. Before that, Paulo had given him a gift—a gift certificate, to be exact, for a tattoo, which LC hadn't used yet. Paulo's torso was close to being covered with them, intricate designs that swirled over muscles in his back and arms and made him that much goddamned harder to resist.

LC loved looking at them, loved tracing them with his tongue, his fingers, watching the way they moved when LC was pounding him, the way he had last night.

"I was glad you came over," Paulo said after they'd finished the appetizers and waited on the next course.

LC had been surprised, too. He'd been restless for months and prowling the club scene no longer held his interest. Crave was sold and things were moving forward.

Everyone was moving forward and he'd been standing still. At first, there had been a lot to do with the sale of the club and the lofts and the construction of the new apartments he and Damon bought, along with the rest of the building. They were now living on opposite ends of the top floor, and the plan was to renovate and rent the rest of the apartments.

There was still a hell of a lot to do, but LC didn't feel

like handling any of it, especially not last night. No, he'd wanted to handle someone, and his car had pointed in the direction of Paulo's place almost as if he'd had no control.

But LC knew that was bullshit.

Paulo had barely been able to get out a hello before LC had him pinned, telling Paulo he'd been dreaming about him before he could stop himself. After that, it was a blur of hands and tongues and *oh yeah*s, and then LC was agreeing to dinner, because he'd just taken the man without so much as a this-is-where-I've-been-for-the-past-few-months explanation.

He'd stayed through until the sun came up and straggled back to his new place, and now he was here, next to this man in this dark restaurant, and he'd been turned on from the time Paulo had picked him up.

If he was honest with himself, Paulo was handling him and LC really fucking liked it.

Paulo hadn't asked him any more about the dreams LC had about him, and for that, LC was grateful. Because this, the tug in the stomach when Paulo looked at him, was new...the first time since Styx, and he knew this man could make him happy, if he allowed it.

He downed the rest of his wine and stood before he told Paulo that. "Headed to the restroom—I'll be back."

"I'd join you, but I have a reputation in this place," Paulo said with a sly smile.

"I'm sure." LC threaded his way through the back

hallway, found the men's room. He pissed and washed up in the private restroom, wiped his hands on a paper towel, and it was all normal. So normal.

Until the lights went out and shots rang out inside the restaurant and an arm came up across his body, a hand over his mouth, and his natural instinct to fight like hell was quelled with a single breath.

Styx. He'd recognize the man's scent—his touch—blindfolded. Many a time he'd actually done so, but this situation was a thousand percent different.

"Not a word." Styx's voice, rough like gravel. Rougher when he was angry or aroused. His breath was warm and minty—Altoids. The man had always been addicted to them.

Damn, you remembered the oddest things when your ass was on the line. And speaking of asses, his was pressed hard to Styx's groin…and the man's arousal was unmistakable. Nice to know he wasn't the only one affected by the close proximity.

He moved his head and Styx took his hand away.

"Paulo," he said, and Styx answered, "Your friend's safe—my associate has him."

Good, that was good, but Jesus, what was going on here?

He heard the slight snick of a gun's safety being released and then heavy footsteps. Whoever was coming wasn't interested in stealth.

Not good.

"Whatever happens, stay put in here. I'll take care of everything." Styx barely mouthed the words but LC heard them loud and clear. And then he was left alone in the dark, and yeah, that was the story of his goddamned life with and without Styx, and he listened and waited.

No more shots, but someone had been killed. LC had been around stealth and death long enough in the Army to the point where he could taste the violence. He'd been on the receiving end of it since birth.

Goddammit, LC, shake that shit off.

And then Styx was back, tugging at him, and LC resisted. "I'm not going anywhere until you tell me what the hell's going on out there."

"There's trouble. Now shut up and do what I say."

"I'm so beyond listening to you."

"You have no idea who and what you're up against. Come with me," Styx said, and LC reluctantly followed him into the restaurant's storeroom, close to the parking lot. And even though it was dark as night inside the restaurant's back room, LC would know the man, could practically see the dark blond hair, longer than it had been, eyes that never failed to mesmerize him, the hard body and even harder cock that had probed him earlier.

LC knew what he was up against—and he was powerless to stop it. And when he started to edge past Styx, Styx let him go at first and then pushed him hard against the wall by the door.

"Are you with that guy?" he whispered into LC's neck, and he wanted to tell Styx not to do that.

Instead, he ground out, "His name is Paulo. And now you're worried about my dating habits?"

"I'm always worried about you."

"The not calling or writing is a great way to show that."

"It's the way it has to be."

Has to be…not using the past tense meant that's what would happen after Styx did whatever it was he needed to here. "What, exactly, is happening out there to get the CIA involved?"

"Can't tell you."

"Right. I don't have the clearance to be involved in any part of your life." Never did. Never would. "Let fucking go of me."

"You can't leave now."

"Then you'll have to arrest me."

With that, Styx reached up and yanked LC's arms down and behind his back, and when the cuffs snicked on his wrists, he cursed bitterly. "Where's Paulo?"

"Safe."

"Not what I asked."

"Are you two serious?"

"Why don't you tell me? You've been spying on me for God knows how long."

"I call it keeping you safe."

"Get. The fuck. Off me."

Styx didn't listen. Never did, which was why the military hadn't been for him. "You bottom for him?"

"I'm trying to figure out why the hell you would care if I did."

"Guess I have my answer. And you know why."

"Not anymore, Styx. Too much time's passed."

He felt Styx's body stiffen, thought the man would release him. And then…

And then Styx's hand went to his cock as he sucked on the back of LC's neck along the spot—*that spot*—he'd discovered drove LC wild.

The only one who'd ever found it, and oh God, he was going to come in his fucking pants if Styx didn't stop.

And Styx would not stop.

"Like that, baby?" Styx whispered after licking the spot where LC knew there'd be a red mark that would stay there for days, then used his tongue and teeth and hands, slipped into LC's half unzipped jeans to work his magic.

"Fuck…please…don't, Styx." But he was saying *don't* and meant *don't stop*. And it was something he wanted—needed—too much to struggle more.

He'd always been a goddamned whore for this man—that would never change.

"Styx." The name, moaned into the dark, and if the man called him by his nickname, he'd lose it in his pants.

A few minutes and then a husky whisper answered, "Yeah, come right now, Law."

Law.

Law had no choice. His body always deferred to Styx's wishes. *Always.*

Styx wiped the man's stomach with some hastily grabbed napkins—he'd pulled Law's shirt up before he came so at least there wasn't a huge mess, and it had taken everything to not get on his knees and let Law come down his throat.

He threw the used napkins aside and fixed Law's clothes as the man remained silent, his breathing calming from the riot it had been moments earlier, when he'd come and cried out Styx's name.

God, he'd been dreaming about that for fucking ever.

"How long have you been checking up on me?" Law asked finally, his voice hoarse.

"Since the second I left your side."

"Right, and that was your damned choice." Law was furious. He slammed Styx off him and Styx hit the wall hard, and he tried to stumble forward.

Too late. Law had him pinned. Law, who had elite training and had gotten the handcuffs off like they'd been paper. Now, his body ground against Styx's. "You're a goddamned coward, running from me. From us."

"You don't understand."

"Then make me," Law demanded. When Styx said

nothing, Law brought his mouth on Styx's in a punishing kiss meant to torment him with memories. His tongue forced itself into Styx's mouth, his cock pressed against Styx's as their groins ground together and finally, Styx brought his hand up to twist in Law's hair, keeping him from breaking the kiss. He tasted like Styx and mint and God, he'd missed this more than he even knew.

This was why he'd stayed away completely. For him, Law was like a drug—addicting and intoxicating, and he was in so much trouble.

He didn't care. Not when Law's hand reached between them and unzipped Styx's jeans so his hard cock slapped unfettered into Law's hand.

Styx groaned against his mouth at the contact, felt Law smile and then his hand stroked his cock in a way that Styx remembered, played with his Prince Albert piercing in a way that made Styx want to scream and fuck him immediately.

Law had always been talented. Now, more so and Styx wanted nothing more than to let him take over completely, to admit everything to him and beg for forgiveness.

He was this close to doing so, especially when Law stroked harder and fast and Styx's balls tightened and his orgasm loomed imminently.

"Fuck…Law." He threw his head back as his hips bucked uncontrollably.

Law could always make him come like this, could always

make him lose control…and love it. Styx wondered if Law felt the same or if the loss of control would make Law angry and retreat back into his shell once the orgasm faded and he regained his senses.

Law didn't clean him or zip him, left Styx to do it himself and when he was done, the lights came up—Tomcat's signal for the all-clear. For now, at least.

The man's real name was Clint, but he hadn't used that in the year and a half he'd been on the sting inside the motorcycle gang's operation. Better that Styx and everyone else used the call sign. Better…and safer.

Law was staring at him, sizing him up. Goddamn, Law looked good. Rugged, sensual…age had done him well. "Law, you've got to let me explain."

"I know what you want. You want control over me. You don't want me, but you've made sure I can't be with anyone else." Law was furious, ten years of pent-up anger tearing into Styx's soul.

He couldn't admit to Law that he'd done it enough to himself. Oftentimes it made him seek escape in whiskey and men until he couldn't see straight. And it never goddamned helped worth a damn.

He reached out to pull Law close, to admit something when they heard more shots. And Styx did grab Law, but only to stop him from running through the restaurant to check on his friend. "Wait—stop," he told the man, and Law consented for a second as Styx called Tomcat.

Tomcat told him, "There's another assassin—get the hell out of there."

"It's okay—everyone's all right," he lied to Law. "We've got to get out of here."

Law leveled him with a gaze, his voice as dangerous as Styx had ever heard when he stated, "Not without Paulo."

When Paulo first heard the shots that rang out from the kitchen, he sprang into action. ID'd himself as a cop, told everyone in the restaurant to get down and stay down under tables or behind the bar and then he pulled his gun and snaked his way through the hallway toward the kitchen. Prayed that LC hadn't gotten caught in the crossfire.

He remained flat against the wall, ready to check the bathroom for LC when he caught sight of a tall man coming down the corridor, toting a gun and flashing his badge. CIA. He motioned for Paulo to duck into the small break room to his right, and he did.

"What's going on?" he asked the agent.

"We have it under control."

"My friend was in the bathroom—"

The agent held up his finger and spoke into the mic on his wrist, then asked, "You Paulo?"

"Yes."

"He's all right. He knows you're okay." He put his arm

down and extended his hand. "Call me Tomcat. Nice work keeping everyone calm out there."

"Do you need me to call the precinct?"

"I'm sure they're coming—right now, we'd prefer to keep this quiet."

Yeah, that was how the feds did things, but Paulo couldn't shake the feeling that the danger hadn't passed. That Tomcat was actually shielding him from something.

Was this man protecting him? "I don't need a bodyguard."

Tomcat simply grinned a little and murmured into the mic on his wrist again. The man was at least six foot-five, with dark hair, tattooed arms and a fierce-looking sawed-off shotgun. Looked like some kind of rogue agent. "You're gonna stay with me anyway."

Paulo didn't answer, and the men remained silent for what seemed like a hell of a long time. Then more shots rang out and he and Tomcat immediately went guns up against either side of the door.

"I'm going—you stay," Tomcat told him.

"Fuck that. What about all the people in the restaurant?"

"You're my concern."

Paulo nodded as if he conceded, because it was faster. Left the room a minute after Tomcat and went in the opposite direction toward the main part of the restaurant. He checked on the patrons, assuring them that he would protect them, making sure no one needed medical attention, because some of them looked like they were in shock.

And then he stilled, because it was too quiet and not at all like a typical aftermath. Whether or not Tomcat was after someone in the kitchen, there was more than one assailant here.

Paulo checked the windows of the restaurant—it was all quiet on the street front, but that wasn't odd. It was a dead-end, out-of-the-way place and the restaurant was the only destination. The parking lot was in the back and there was only one front entrance from the street.

But there was another doorway to the right—no doubt to a back staircase. Paulo saw the knob turn and then a man came barreling out from where he'd been lying in wait.

And he was staring right at Paulo. Gunning for him.

Paulo didn't wait to ask how long he'd been there, aimed and pulled the trigger twice, took the bastard down without hesitation.

He'd learned his lesson once, the hard way—hesitation cost you—and, if you were lucky, it was only your pride.

"It's okay," he told the patrons, went to the downed man with his gun still drawn, kicked the gun away from the body and knelt to take a pulse.

There was none. Paulo felt for his ID and pulled out a couple of photographs instead.

The first was a picture of him leaving the hospital, dated three months earlier, according to the back. The next showed LC in the hospital, sleeping in his bed, and a piece of paper had the name of the restaurant and the time of their reservation on it.

This had been an ordered hit.

The thought that he and LC were being targeted churned his stomach, and he continued to roust the dead man until Tomcat was hauling him to his feet and sirens sounded in the background.

"Jesus, but you don't listen."

Paulo jerked out of his grasp and checked his cell phone, pulled out the battery and found no bugs, but that didn't matter—they could've triangulated the signal some other way. He turned it off just in case it was sending out a signal as Tomcat checked out the dead man on the floor.

"Please, help my husband."

Paulo turned immediately to help the older gentleman who was having trouble breathing. The air smelled like gunpowder and was thick with fear, and Paulo got the man flat with his feet up as his wife gave him his heart meds under his tongue.

In a minute, the man's color came back and Paulo allowed Tomcat to move him away.

"Where's LC?" he demanded as Tomcat waved the paramedics in to help. Two men in suits—more obvious agents than Tomcat—came in behind them, presumably to smooth over the situation.

"You're a pain in the goddamned ass," Tomcat muttered to him as they walked toward the kitchen. Paulo saw the blood spatter but he wanted to see LC for himself and that was more important than investigating right at the moment.

"Listen, cop—"

"Detective."

Tomcat stopped in the middle of the hallway. "Whatever. Look, this is a bad situation."

"That guy was an assassin," Paulo said, and Tomcat stared at him as Paulo shoved the pictures into his hands. "He was gunning for me before I'd even turned around. My picture was in his goddamned pocket. Mine and LC's. So don't goddamned bullshit me anymore."

Tomcat put his hands up as if in surrender, told him, "I'm going to put you in the kitchen with your friend and another agent. Think you can stay put and stop being a hero long enough to get an explanation?"

Paulo stared at him, trying to determine if that was sarcasm, and saw nothing but respect in the man's eyes. It might make things easier, but this was far from over.

After Law refused to leave, there were two more shots that practically had him clawing at the door. He'd even tried to take Styx's gun to go out there but Styx held him back and listened on the mic as Tomcat kept him up to date.

Apparently, the cop was suddenly a hero—and

completely fucked at the same time. He'd discovered the hit out on him and Law…the only thing he didn't know was that Styx was the main target.

If Styx had his way, no one beyond him and Tomcat would ever know that part. But it was far too late to keep the secret that his father was also after Law, and Paulo now, by default. The only one he would keep was the fact that his father didn't want him back into the fold this time—no, the man wanted him dead.

"Where's Paulo? I want to see him," Law demanded.

"Fine." Styx gritted his teeth and muttered to Tomcat using the mic on his wrist. "Bring him in here."

It only took a minute before Tomcat was ushering Paulo in, the towheaded man looking more handsome than Styx remembered.

Paulo looked more than pissed, glared at Styx as he went to Law who was barreling toward him too. "You all right?"

The complete concern on both their parts was impossible to miss and threatened to overwhelm him, and he almost turned away when Law tugged Paulo into his arms, murmured, "Jesus, I'm fine. Heard the shots."

"Good." Paulo looked over Law's shoulder at Styx, his eyes held questions but he didn't say anything else.

"Can we get out of here and go home?" Law turned to ask Styx.

"No." Styx glanced at Tomcat who then slipped out of the room, no doubt to get the safe house directive in order, because what would happen next would not be pleasant for any of them. "These men are dangerous."

"And they're after us?" Law asked.

"They're after you because of me. They followed me to your hospital room and they've been tailing you ever since," Styx admitted.

"Why?" Law demanded, ignoring the part about the hospital visit, which made Styx's gut tighten. What had he expected, Law to run into his arms with that admission?

"Because they know that the best way to get to me is through someone I love."

Paulo stared between the two of them as he remained in Law's arms—because Law was holding on to him tightly. "You're the one who left him for years."

"You're the one who'll leave before the year's out, if your stay-in-one-place-for-two-years-or-less pattern holds. Or is Law the love of your life? The one who'll make you stay, even if it means trouble?"

Paulo turned back to Law. "At least now I know your first name. But that doesn't mean I don't get to tie you down."

Paulo almost smiled at the growl the blond man named Styx emitted after his comment about tying LC down.

Law. Granted, Paulo had known LC's real name was Lawrence Connor because he'd investigated his past—he'd just been waiting for LC to tell Paulo himself and it had killed him not to be able to use it. And that asshole CIA guy was probably the only one LC let call him that. So yeah, the pleasure at the zing was short-lived because he was the one getting screwed in this situation.

Law. It suited the handsome man whose hair was a darker blond than both his and Styx's.

He wasn't even touching Styx's comment regarding his past. Styx, who was glaring between him and Law, even as Law gave him a small grin. "It's a deal."

"I hate to interrupt this magic moment," Styx started, and Paulo broke away from Law, fisted his hands and went toe-to-toe with Styx. The agent was a few inches taller than he was, but Paulo had taken on bigger and badder in his time, and he wasn't going to let this motherfucker think Paulo would kowtow to him.

"Then don't."

"Got yourself a bodyguard, Law?" Styx asked with a grin Paulo itched to punch off his face.

Law stepped in between them, his hand on Paulo's shoulder, tugging him back even as Paulo demanded, "Why aren't we getting the hell out of here if it's so dangerous?"

"Look, cop—"

Paulo knew it was time to push Styx. "If I don't start hearing an explanation now, I'm calling my precinct."

"Try it," Styx told him through gritted teeth.

"Come on, Paulo. We'll figure it out," Law told him, and

Paulo turned from Styx back to him. He was grateful Law was safe and in one piece, and wasn't ready to tell him about the photos in the assassin's pocket. Styx would have to let them both in on everything soon enough, and Law already looked wrecked.

"There's nothing to figure out—you'll listen to me and do what I say," Styx persisted, and Paulo didn't have to worry about punching the shit out of Styx, because Law was mad enough for both of them.

"What the hell are we supposed to do now? Hide out in some shithole until you catch whoever's shooting at us?" Law demanded, no doubt partly to distract him from the pissing contest he appeared to be in with Paulo.

Styx eyed him coolly. "Yes. Tell the cop to give me his phone. And then I'm taking both of you into protective custody."

Law shook his head. "You've got to be kidding me. What—now we're going into witness protection for reasons unknown? Bullshit."

"I know the reasons." Styx's eyes met Paulo's and the two men came to a silent agreement. "Like I said, I've been trying to avoid this for months."

"Why's it taken that long? Oh, wait, that's SOP for the CIA," Law muttered. "Who got killed here tonight?"

"You don't have the clearance for that intel," Styx told him, and Paulo watched the fireworks between these men with great interest. The tension there was extreme—sexual and otherwise, and Paulo couldn't believe he was stuck in the middle of them.

"So let me get this straight—the three of us have to hole up together so we don't get killed?" Paulo asked, and Styx nodded, looking as grim at that prospect as Paulo felt. "For how long?"

"As long as it takes."

"I am going to need way more of an explanation than that, Styx." Law ran a hand through his hair, his irritation mounting as evidenced by the tension in his shoulders. Paulo put a hand on one of them, because no matter what, Law was safe for now.

"We can't hang around here to discuss this," Styx told him. "I'll tell you more when we get someplace a little less public, all right?"

"You weren't worried about that earlier," Law growled, and Paulo made a mental note to find out what that was all about, but first he put his hand on Law's arm.

"There was an assassin I shot. He had pictures of us in his pocket," he told Law, who stared between him and Styx.

Paulo actually felt bad for the agent, because Styx looked at Law the way Paulo felt…and why would you stay away from someone you loved so damned much?

None of this made sense, but it appeared he'd have nothing but time on his hands to unravel it.

2

Law was practically vibrating with frustration and his mind was swimming in questions, but he forced himself into soldier mode to tamp it all down.

If assassins had come here to take him out—and Paulo—then it was time to let the CIA do its job. He could worry about kicking Styx's ass later. Right now, getting Paulo someplace safe and finding out what he'd had to do out there was top priority.

"I need both your phones before we move," Styx reiterated to him. Law pulled it out of his pocket and caught a text message from Damon. He scrolled through to see a *we're here safe and sound* message.

When he looked up at Styx, the man relented a little as if reading his mind. "Worried about Damon?"

"He's away for a couple of weeks—Europe," Law admitted, because he wouldn't worry Damon about this while he was taking a well-deserved vacation with Tanner. "I'll just text him back now, but I'll need to check in with emails and a call at some point, too."

Styx nodded and Law finished a quick text to Damon, grateful he didn't have to face his friend directly, and then handed over his phone.

He turned his attention back to Paulo. It must be hard for him to stand there and do nothing, especially after what happened in the restaurant, but he was handling himself well under the pressure. Because of their various backgrounds dealing with all types of violence and mayhem, none of them did vulnerable or flying blind well, but Law trusted Styx. Of course, he understood why Paulo didn't.

"I'll need your gun and your badge, too," Styx told Paulo, the command in his voice unmistakable, and Law tried to forget about the hand jobs they'd given each other.

Because if he could forget, he wouldn't have to admit it to Paulo. Normally, he'd go by the code of say nothing, but that wasn't going to work in this situation.

"I can't just not show up for work, asshole. I'm not getting fired because of you," Paulo said, but he did hand Styx his badge and then his gun with the safety on.

Law could smell that it had been recently fired. Paulo saved his life—probably many others inside the restaurant as well. "He's right, Styx."

Styx looked at Paulo for a long, hard minute. "I'll get you a throw-away phone in the morning. As for work, you'll have to take leave."

"I'm not taking a leave of absence. Who the fuck are you and why did that man have us in his sights?" he asked Styx, but Law pulled him back.

"You need to explain this," he told his former lover.

Styx's partner came back then, just in time to step in between Styx and Paulo. "Dial it down, you two. Detective, cut the shit and hand over the phone. Styx will explain more once you get to a safe location, and I shouldn't have to explain this kind of SOP to a cop. You're on a need-to-know basis for now. In other news, the safe house won't be ready till morning. Tonight, you get a beautiful motel by the airport. In the next state. And extra ammo. Sorry, but this is the way it has to be, at least for now. Your lives are on the line. The CIA doesn't hide people for nothing."

That was the truth, and while it sent a chill through Law, it seemed to calm Paulo down, at least for the moment. Styx took that opportunity to usher all of them into a waiting truck while Tomcat remained inside the restaurant.

"I don't like this any more than you do," Law told Paulo after opening the back door for him.

Paulo got in next to him, sat close by and Law fought a ridiculous urge to hold his hand.

"Fuck, I'm sorry," was all he said.

"Not your fault." Still, Paulo's voice—his bearing—was tight. "You trust him?"

"I do. He wouldn't hurt me." Even as he spoke those words, he heard Paulo's laugh and knew how fucking ridiculous he sounded. "He won't hurt us like that. He's got to be telling the truth."

"Yeah, feds never lie."

"He wouldn't put my life in danger. I'll get the truth from him." He ran a hand along Paulo's thigh, heard Paulo's soft snort in the dark.

Paulo finally handed Law his phone. "This definitely wasn't the date I had planned."

Styx bristled at Paulo's mention of his date with Law. Maybe Paulo would want to know what his date had done tonight with Styx but hell, he wouldn't be that much of a prick.

Not yet, anyway.

And then Law handed Styx Paulo's phone and Styx pocketed it and made a mental note to hand it over to Tomcat in the morning. Right after he checked it out to make sure nothing suspicious showed, although really, Styx was almost positive the young detective had nothing to do with what was happening in his life.

No, that had been his own doing. He checked the rearview, caught a glimpse of Paulo looking back at him. The two men would be circling each other in a pissing contest—one that had already started back inside the restaurant.

What a clusterfuck. Styx's hands could tremble just thinking about how close he'd come to losing Law, and he was glad he could grip the wheel to steady them. A few seconds later and Law would've been in the hallway and in the shooter's sights.

As it was, an innocent man had been shot—according to Tomcat, the EMTs got him to the hospital in time—he was in surgery and expected to live. And now Styx had Law— safe and sound and all kinds of angry, in the backseat, plus some unexpected baggage.

Paulo was a beautiful man—not a twink, no, he was hard-edged, masculine and a goddamned suspicious bastard. Protective of Law, too, and while Styx appreciated that, he'd appreciate Paulo getting his hands off Law even more.

Law's not yours anymore. And Styx had no right to expect him to wait around, but a big part of him hoped he had. And Law had, at least until three months ago when he'd called Styx and told him he was done—and then he'd nearly gotten himself killed and Styx had gotten his head out of his ass and went to the hospital.

That was when he'd found Paulo by Law's side.

With that single visit, he'd brought Armageddon down on their heads, although it had always hovered there. Styx just hadn't realized how close, and that chilled him.

He'd left Law to keep him out of danger, but that danger had never stopped lurking around Law, looking for another way inside. It found it and now Paulo was in danger too, by association.

Paulo, a cop with a lost-boy past…a smile that made Styx hard and he guessed Law as well—and it appeared he'd found a way to make Law happy.

And Styx had fucked it up again.

Law knew that the walls of this shithole would close in on all of them before the twenty-four hour mark. They'd driven for hours—he noted they'd crossed into Virginia. There was still a chill in the air, despite the promise of spring just around the corner, when Styx ushered them into the block of rooms.

He'd actually called it a suite, but it was just two motel rooms with doors opened between them located near the airport. Each room had one double bed, a chair and not much else. Considering the men only had the clothes on their backs and some sodas Styx had grabbed at the vending machine when he'd checked them in, these conditions were Spartan at best, reminded Law of his Delta days.

Except then he'd had weapons and plans. Now, he had no real explanations and a lot of pent-up anger he was trying hard to control in order to keep Paulo from flipping.

"A better place tomorrow," Styx assured them, which was really no assurance at all.

"You'd better get the full story from him," Paulo muttered to Law.

"I'm right here, you know," Styx said.

"Then start talking." Paulo moved toward Styx and Law, once again, stepped in.

"Start talking, Styx. This is bullshit."

"I said, tomorrow." Styx growled the words and went to work on securing the first door from the inside before heading to the second room and doing the same there, propping the back of it with a chair pressed to the knob. He also put up some kind of alarm, strung along the top of the doorjamb.

Paulo moved to the doorway that separated the rooms, was watching Styx carefully. Law wanted nothing more than to pull Paulo into bed with him, but he knew the younger man had too much anger, too many questions for that. He needed to get them out of this room and away from Styx. Styx, who threw himself on the bed in the first room and stretched out shamelessly. He'd strip next—Law was sure of it, and so Law tugged Paulo through the opening of the second room and said, "Take the bed, Paulo."

Paulo stared at him and then surprised him by asking, "You joining me or him?"

"You, if there's an invite."

Styx snorted from the other room. "The Law I knew didn't ask—he'd take what he wanted."

"He does—trust me on that." Paulo managed to not sound the least bit defensive.

That would shut Styx up for maybe five minutes. But

Law had just as many questions as they all did and the most right to know the answers.

"He's here because of you, and he's got to stay here because of you, so deal with him listening in," he told Styx.

"Not tonight," Styx called.

Why, when Law dreamed of this man, did he not recall what a complete pain in the ass he could be—because he'd always been, most definitely.

"Keep the door open," Styx said but Law slammed it closed as he spoke. Styx didn't come to open it and Law turned and found Paulo waiting, watching him carefully.

None of them would be getting any sleep—and having sex seemed doubtful—and man, this was going to be a long-assed night.

Paulo leaned against the dresser that held a small TV and watched Law wrestle with his feelings. He could practically hear the wheels turning, as he had the entire car ride here when none of them spoke and Styx had turned the music up to ensure they wouldn't have to.

There was so much goddamned tension—sexual, emotional—that Paulo wanted to punch his fist through the wall, but that would solve nothing.

His innate ability to read people helped him tremendously in both his career and his personal life. And although, just like Law, Styx had his brick walls built high around him, there was one thing that was crystal clear. Styx pined for Law as much as Law had for him—Paulo could see it easily in the agent's eyes. Which meant that this threesome was about to get a hell of a lot more interesting.

When he sized up Styx in the restaurant, he could immediately understand why Law would wait for this man, how Styx could ruin him for others. Tall, broad, ruggedly handsome, his energy was like a punch to the gut and somehow still mesmerizingly pleasurable.

Law had never promised Paulo anything but sex and then finally dinner, but in light of the current situation, Paulo knew all bets were off. Tonight, their bed would be crowded as hell, and Paulo was pretty sure in this case, three wouldn't be company.

Especially when he'd planned on having Law all to himself again tonight, because the man goddamned owed him.

Paulo had never expected him to show again—let alone at midnight last night, but that's exactly what had happened. He'd been about to pop in *The Transporter 2* when the banging started—his first thought went to Law, because not too many people could bypass the lock on the main front door that easily.

He'd opened it to find the man standing there, looking as damned good as always. "Let me in."

"Fuck you." Paulo held the door so there was no way

Law could enter except by kicking the door down, and you know what—he wouldn't put it past him.

"Yeah. Come on, Paulo."

His body started up the second the man started talking.

"I'm an idiot," he muttered but Law reached through the door and put a finger under his chin. "No, not you. Me."

Paulo stared into the truth in those blue eyes, which also held an apology.

"Please, Paulo, let me in all the way," Law implored, and whether he was asking Paulo to open the door to his apartment or something more, it didn't matter.

He was asking, and Paulo relented, released his grip on the door, allowing Law to come inside and gather Paulo in his arms.

"Where've you been?" was asked as Law's mouth was on his. And then Law mentioned his dreams between kisses that were nearly punishing in their need.

Paulo's clothes were off and he'd found himself on his back on his mattress as Law showed him just how much he missed him. Showed him with his mouth and tongue and teeth and touch, showed him when he refused to take his eyes from Paulo, even when they both came to a shuddering climax.

"Hope you didn't have plans," Law said, pressing himself against Paulo.

"I was going to watch a movie."

"Want me to leave?"

"No."

"Good."

They never made it more than a quarter of a way through the film, no matter how many times they started it, and neither man cared.

Looking at Law now, as he wrestled with everything, Paulo couldn't help but wonder what would've happened if Styx hadn't barreled back into Law's life and left this wreckage in his wake.

But even as Paulo was angered by that, he knew Styx was hurting, that this was the last thing he'd wanted to do to Law.

Fate always had a way of intervening. Pushed everyone in the right direction. The thing with fate though, was that someone always got hurt. Paulo knew that this time, it would be him. So for the time being, he'd climb into bed with Law and take comfort in Law's body close to his for as long as he had the man

"What's the deal with this guy?" he asked finally.

"Styx has no memory of his childhood before the age of sixteen. This has to have something to do with his past."

"And somehow, the man with our picture in his pocket is connected to Styx?"

"When Styx left, he never told me why. I haven't seen him for ten years. Even before that, I only saw him a few times from when we were nineteen until I turned twenty-four."

"When you saw him again, how did you not demand an answer?" Paulo asked but he knew, judging by the flush on Law's face that their reunion had consisted of fucking until the sun came up and Styx no doubt leaving before that to avoid talking.

"I knew he was in the CIA. Knew that, even without an explanation of what had happened, his job could keep us apart. I always assumed his family had something to do with his memory, his disappearance, but he could never find out anything about his past. After a while, he stopped looking and things were okay." He stared at Paulo for a long moment. "When he came to live with us, he didn't even remember his name. He doesn't know his own damned name."

Law's voice grew hoarse for a second. His description of Styx's life made Paulo think slightly differently of the tall man alone in the other room—and Paulo knew what he needed to do.

Still it made his heart ache to have to push Law away, but it was what was best for him. "Go talk to Styx—now."

"No. Not tonight."

"He wants to tell you, but I can't blame him for not wanting to talk in front of me, even if it's affecting my life. Go to him—shut the door and talk. I'll be fine."

All Law could say was, "Paulo."

But Paulo pulled back, and he was being far more mature than he wanted to be. "You're confused."

"Yes."

"I'm not the one you want in your bed tonight."

"Is that permission?"

"More like realism."

"I'm sorry—about all of this," Law told him.

"I knew you loved someone else, remember?"

"I don't want you giving up on us."

"Us? What us is there?" Paulo asked, but there wasn't any rancor in his tone. How could there be? "Styx is the love of your life and you only get one, if you're lucky."

"Paulo, wait—"

"What? You're going to tell me we can still be friends?"

"Styx won't stick around."

"Oh, so I'm your back-up."

"No." Law yanked Paulo to him hard. "You are not that at all. You're the first man I've been with more than once since Styx, ten years ago. That's how *non*-back-up you are."

He brought his mouth down on Paulo's, hard and punishing, wouldn't let up till Paulo responded, which he couldn't help but do. His hands fisted at his sides as he tried not to grab and touch Law, lick him up and down the way he wanted to, until Law couldn't remember his own name, never mind Styx's.

But after a long moment of resisting, he lifted his arms and wrapped them around Law, pushing him back against the wall and taking some of the control he so desperately craved in this situation.

Surprisingly, Law didn't resist at all, let Paulo press him, grind against him, kiss him deeply until both were breathing heavily. He wondered how fast he could undress Law, if he could hold his arms above his head, spread his legs and fuck him…if he wanted that or if he wanted Law to fill him.

Law's hands were on his ass, pulling Paulo closer, the friction delicious and could send them both over the edge like a couple of teenagers dry humping in their car. Paulo's skin felt too tight, his muscles taut and God, he wanted to come. Needed to.

"Fuck yeah," he murmured against the man's mouth.

"Yes."

It would be so easy to do this, to sink to the floor, strip naked and just screw until he blotted everything out. But that wasn't going to solve anything and he'd let Law fuck away their problems too many times in their short time together.

He backed off, tearing himself away, leaving Law with swollen lips, a flushed face and a hard-on. "You need to find out everything. For your safety."

"Yours too."

"This is between you and Styx."

Paulo had almost felt sorry for Styx earlier because he caught a glimpse of the quick flash of pain in Styx's eyes, and the way he looked at Law…dammit, it was the way Paulo had always wanted someone to look at him.

At times, like last night, he'd thought he'd caught Law looking at him with more than simple lust but he'd convinced himself it was a trick of the light.

Noting the way Law looked at Styx, Paulo knew he'd been right.

There was no fighting this. He was sending Law to Styx and he had no doubt they'd end up in bed together. The fact that it stung was his problem. "Go to him."

Law leaned his head against the wall and drew a deep breath. Fixed his shirt, adjusted his balls and ran his hands through his hair. After a few more moments of letting his arousal wind down, he pushed off and headed to the door that adjoined the rooms.

He looked back at Paulo one last time, grimaced, like it was painful to leave, and Paulo wanted to believe it was.

"Go now, LC."

"Law," he said firmly. "I want you to call me Law."

Paulo bit back a smart-ass remark and told him quietly, "Okay, Law, go."

"I like the way you say it," Law said, just as quietly, and then he left to go to Styx.

3

Okay, Law, go.

With Paulo's voice enmeshed in his mind, Law opened the door and walked into Styx's room without knocking. Caught between his present and his past, he couldn't shake the feeling that his future lay somewhere in between.

Styx lay on his back on the bed staring at the ceiling, just as Law had left him. The man had rarely slept when they were younger and Law saw nothing had changed. If anything, Styx's job probably exacerbated his insomnia.

"You're done with the boy that quickly and quietly?" Styx smirked.

"Ah, fuck off. And he's not a boy."

"You tell him that I already got you off tonight?"

Coming in here had been a mistake. "I won't hurt him—and I won't let you."

"You're serious about him."

"We haven't been together long," Law said, surprised the word *together* came out of his mouth that easily, surprised that he didn't deny anything.

"But you like him," Styx persisted.

"He's the first man I've been with more than once since you," he admitted, and Styx just stared at him. "What? That makes me an idiot, right? Because I'm sure you've had your share of relationships."

"Ah, Law, come on. There's been no one worth shit since you. You have to know that," Styx said softly.

"I don't know what to make of anything."

"It hasn't been easy on me either. You gotta believe that. All these years, and you had Damon. I was alone, by necessity. But it still hurt."

"By choice," Law insisted as he sat on the edge of the bed, where Styx still lay on his back. "I would've gone with you. Hell, Damon might've too, or you could've stayed and we could've figured a way out of whatever it was together."

"I always thought…" Styx shook his head. "Forget it."

"What?"

"I thought we had forever. A stupid kid's dream."

"It wasn't stupid. I wanted that, too." Law paused. "What happened?"

"My past showed, and the only way to keep you and Damon safe was to leave. It was the only way, or I'd never have stayed apart from you." Styx sat up for a moment, moved closer to press his face to Law's shoulder. "You have to believe me."

"I do believe you. But you had sixteen years to tell me. I deserve an explanation," Law said quietly, and Styx didn't dispute that but he still didn't jump right into the story.

"Why did Paulo let you sneak away?"

"He's the one who told me to come in here. He knew you would rather talk to me in private."

Styx snorted but he didn't say anything more, just moved away to lie down again. This time, Law joined him, lying on his side to face Styx.

"You sure you're ready for this?" Styx asked.

"Since the second I met you," Law told him, and Styx smiled but it was short-lived.

"The more you know, the more danger for both of you," Styx said. "Shit, you have no idea…been keeping you safe for sixteen years…for nothing."

"Tell me. Come on…there's too much history between us."

"My memory," he started, then stopped just as abruptly.

"You remember?"

"Not exactly. But someone's been filling in the blanks for me. And now I've got a few more pieces of puzzle, including my birth certificate."

Styx looked haunted, and so wiped that Law didn't want to make him continue. He'd always wanted to protect Styx from all the dark spaces in his own brain. Wanted to protect Styx from everything.

And so he drew Styx's mouth to his, kissed him so well the present melded into the past and they were teens on a twin bed, exploring something beyond simply fucking for the first time. If it was possible to go back in time, they were there, with nothing stopping them from fucking and spending every waking moment together. Styx's tongue played with his, and Law pushed Styx back and climbed on him, wanting him with an immediacy that couldn't be helped.

Styx's hands tangled in his hair when Law straddled him and Law ground his jean-clad cock against Styx's, hearing the moans from the man under him. God, it would be so easy to erase all their pain, to fall back into Styx, to run away with him.

Except it wasn't both of them alone. There was Paulo now...and there were sixteen years of explanations needed.

There was so damned much to figure out. And so he pulled away from Styx reluctantly, then just pressed his forehead to the other man's for a long moment.

"Tell me everything, Styx," he urged hoarsely.

The problem was, Styx still didn't remember everything. Or really, anything—he was still working off of another person's word, another person's threats.

But that person called himself his father, and Styx looked so much like him, it left little room for doubt. "My father found me three months ago. And it's not the first time."

"Then he's the reason you took off in the first place."

God, Law looked so hurt when he spoke those words, and that had been the last thing Styx intended, then and now.

His friend and former lover looked the same—the few lines here and there did nothing to diminish his looks—a handsome fucking angel who'd always been there for him.

Styx looked toward the door and wondered what the hell Paulo was thinking in there alone, knowing Law was in here with his ex.

Avoidance was futile. If they were going to be locked up together indefinitely, he'd have to come clean to Law. If Paulo wanted to know, he could hear it from Law. But Styx could barely tell the man he loved, let alone a practical stranger.

Except Paulo didn't seem like such a stranger to him. Which was disturbing and fascinating at the same time.

"Styx." Law put his hand on Styx's shoulder to bring him back to the story, and he launched into the explanation without further delay.

"It started the night Damon was attacked. He went out and you and I stayed home. When two in the morning rolled around and he hadn't checked in, you went looking for him and I stayed home in case he called. Fuck, there are so many nights I wished I'd never stayed home to get that call."

The voice on the other end of Styx's phone was low and controlled…and it had made him go rigid with fear, although he hadn't recognized it.

His body recognized it, even though his mind hadn't.

"Boy, you need to get your ass home or the fag you've been fucking gets cut into little pieces."

He swallowed. "I haven't been fucking anyone."

A short laugh had been followed by a thorough description of Law, including exactly what he'd been wearing when he'd left the house to find Damon an hour before.

"I'm coming."

"Good."

Something…someone was catching up to him, the blind fear was second only to the near-crippling anger. And so he'd packed his shit up and he'd left—his only thought was to keep Law safe.

Now, Law's face paled and his jaw tightened as understanding dawned. "He'd been following us."

"Yeah. He'd known where I was for a while—maybe the whole time I was at Greg's. I never bothered to ask because it didn't matter anymore. I was causing trouble for everyone, especially you, and so before I hung up, he gave me an address and instructions on what to do when I got there."

The address was Upper East Side, a door-manned building. He'd slid past when a woman exited and the doorman was distracted by calling a cab for her, used the stairs and made it up to the sixth-floor apartment.

He didn't know who the guy was or what he'd done—all he

knew was that his father would make good on his promise to hurt Law, knew it deep in his bones. When the man answered the door, Styx pushed his way inside and beat the shit out of the guy. Forced him to give up his safe combination and then Styx cleaned out the money and left the apartment and the building and met his father in Central Park.

It had been like looking in a mirror—Styx knew what he'd age into, although his father didn't appear to be older than forty, if that. He'd looked strangely relaxed as he'd stared at Styx and Styx fought the urge to ask him to fill in the blanks about his life and memories.

He decided that ignorance was bliss. "Until I contacted the police, who in turn got me hooked up with the FBI and finally the CIA, I had no idea my father was such a wanted man."

"Who is he?"

"An assassin who freelances for most of the major mafias—mainly in the US but he's done hits abroad as well. They'd been trying to catch him for years, but the CIA didn't even know where he lived."

"What did the CIA know about him?"

"His name. They never knew he'd had a son. There were no records of me anywhere—not until the other night. Before I saw the birth certificate, I didn't know for sure he'd resurfaced or if I was truly his son. My memory's still a total fucking blank. And I wasn't about to ask the old man anything." Styx laughed, but there was no humor behind it.

"What about your mother?"

"I never asked—he never said." Styx stared at the wall instead of Law. "If she's alive and she escaped from him, she's better off staying away from me. If she knows what happened to me…"

Then who'd want to know her anyway? "I look like him. He calls me kid. *Hey, kid, aren't you gonna give your old man a hug*?" Styx shuddered. Law was the only man he could ever let his guard down around and he knew it would be okay. "I didn't tell him I'd lost my memory—it didn't matter. We never took a walk down memory lane. He just gave me jobs and I killed people. I don't know if they were good or bad, but I do know that I'll spend the rest of my life trying to make up for it."

"You did that for me, Styx. Jesus."

"No," he protested vehemently. "Don't you try to take that on yourself. It was my choice. Nothing I did was your fault. I'd do anything to keep you safe. Always will."

"Do you still have the dreams?" Law asked.

He did—the ones where he was running in the fog, surrounded by the blaring horns and then came the sounds of screams…

He always woke up when the screaming started. "I've tried everything—hypnosis, drugs, psychiatrists. I've taken advantage of everything the CIA had to offer and nothing." He dragged his hand through his hair, frustrated at himself the way he always got when he thought about his lack of memory.

"Greg always said it had to have been a major trauma."

"You lived through something God-awful, and you didn't block out your entire memory."

"I wanted to," Law admitted. "So the CIA took you in because they thought you'd eventually remember."

Styx nodded. "At first, I was simply a witness but then they trained me. I worked undercover for the CIA, continuing to play my father's game for two months in order to gather more evidence. He was a wanted man, Law, and I knew a lot of his secrets after working with him. But then he disappeared completely—went off the grid and stopped contacting me. I thought it was over—that he'd gotten killed. But we never stopped looking for him." Styx wanted to turn away but Law wouldn't have allowed that.

Law always thought Styx was the strong one—he'd been so very wrong about that.

"He resurfaced after four years—the SAS clued us in and I knew he'd make contact. When he did, I was finally able to catch him. He went to prison, and for a while, I was free. Working for the CIA, trying to make up for everything my father did."

"That's why you visited me those few times."

"I did, right after he went to jail. But even then, I was worried—he's good, and I knew escape was inevitable. He bided his time in jail for ten years. He escaped three months ago and started following me. The CIA thinks he had help from another country's agency. But the upshot is, he's out. And he's made contact with me. He gave me your address. Old and new." He left out the part about the hit on him because that was something Law didn't need to know yet, if ever. Law would assume that Styx's father wanted him back in the family business, not dead.

Styx would have to leave Law and Paulo behind soon, because they were actually in more danger with him around than without.

But he couldn't leave yet—he needed more time, and he refused to let his father rob him of this little piece of it, no matter how small or ill-timed.

Law cradled Styx's face in his hands. "It's going to be okay."

"It's not. He's never stopped tailing you in an attempt to find me."

The thought that his father had been so close to Law made him so angry and scared at the same time.

"I can take care of myself. I know how to fight dirty."

Styx pushed off the bed and stood. "If I hadn't visited you…if I hadn't been so stupid…"

"I wondered…I felt you there at the hospital, but blamed it on the meds and wishful thinking."

"You didn't seem all that surprised when I mentioned it earlier," he said, and Law's expression softened momentarily. "You'd called and I got worried."

"It was only a matter of time before he did something

to try to pull you back in," Law said fiercely. "If he's known where I was, he would've used me. Maybe this way it was better—we have a chance to stop him."

"There is no *we* in this situation," Styx told him. "I'm in charge of keeping you safe—this is an op, Law, not us against the world."

"You do not get to do this to me again."

"Damn right I do. This isn't up for discussion."

"Nothing's changed, has it? Memories or no memories, you're still the same selfish asshole you always were."

"I did it for you."

"No, you did it for you. You never gave me a choice when we were nineteen, and I'm damned well not giving you the opportunity to take it away again now."

Law knew there was more to the story, but pushing Styx on such a potentially explosive topic wasn't smart. He still had the amnesia. Triggering a memory under any circumstances was problematic, but under these, it could prove deadly.

"You don't know what I did. What kind of guy I was. What if what you know is only what you think you know? I might not be who you think I am."

Styx looked so troubled at his own words that Law could hardly stand it. "I know enough," he told Styx fiercely.

"I'm dangerous."

"So am I."

Styx pushed away. "You and Paulo should hide. Away from me."

"No."

"I'm not giving you the choice."

"I'm through letting you push me away for my own good. That's just as dangerous and it's obviously not working." Styx was protecting him again—the fucking asshole.

"I've been ruining your life for ten years."

"Don't flatter yourself," Law scoffed, the truth of that statement hitting him harder than it should, because although he'd never considered his pining for Styx something that ruined him, he'd definitely been pining. Hoping. Waiting, like a fucking girl.

Jesus Christ.

It had taken ten years—actually, sixteen if he counted when Styx originally left—to open himself up. "I wasn't ready to settle down—the military wasn't exactly conducive to that. And then I was running the club and got all the ass I needed," Law continued.

All excuses he'd used on himself thousands of times, and no, Styx wasn't buying them either.

"You needed to just let me go. I'm sure Damon told you so over the years."

Damon had, constantly, and Law tried, but no one had ever really fit. Greg would've understood. Greg, who'd once told him that Styx reminded him of himself the most of the three boys.

"I was a goddamned mouthy know-it-all. Hid a lot of shit that way," Greg told him.

"But you're not like that now."

"I've got no more shit to hide."

Greg was also single during the time Law knew him. He never brought any guys back to the house—for him, that was off-limits. But he also never dated anyone seriously.

"What about a man for you?" Law asked him once and Greg smiled and told him, "There was someone. Once you've been with the best man…why bother to look for lightning to strike twice?"

For Law, Styx had been that elusive man—still was, but with Paulo, Law had managed to recapture parts of himself he'd thought he'd lost. Parts he'd figured would never be alive again.

But now, he had Styx back with his pierced dick, and Law remembered how it felt inside him, hitting his prostate, turning and rubbing, and holy Mother of God, he could still get hard in an instant thinking about it. That feeling had been the only reason that made him attempt to bottom again with a guy with a Prince Albert, but that had ended in disaster, because the sex hadn't been nearly as good… and because Law had called out Styx's name like a fucking amateur.

This too could end in disaster, for so many different

reasons, the least of which being that he was so angry.

"I was getting everything together," Law said as he pushed off the bed and stood, as did Styx. They started to circle one another as if gearing up for a fight.

"Ten years later," Styx goaded, although he looked sad and Law didn't care, lunged for him so their bodies slammed against the wall.

His was a red-hot anger built on years of waiting for and wanting something he couldn't have. Styx got it—he knew Styx had wanted him, too, but to find out now that Styx was planning on controlling him in this situation the way he'd been controlling him for years was too much to bear.

"Law, calm the fuck down," Styx warned, gave a soft grunt as Law's fist connected with his gut.

Law could always fight—Delta Force had taught him just as much as the CIA had taught Styx. He pinned Styx as best he could, although the upper hand didn't last long. The one with the most anger always lost and tonight, Law was that man.

Styx ended up with Law on his stomach under him, the way they'd ended up so many times before this. But it was hazy, fraught with too many memories of other men, of fucking and drinking too much, of combat and good times and bad.

Styx yanked Law's shirt up roughly, ran his tongue down his spine, a hot line of fire that made Law squirm, even as Styx held him in place with a hand on the back of Law's neck, his cheek pressed to the ground.

"I wreck you, Law. I hate that."

"Do I wreck you? Do you stay up nights thinking about me? Remembering what it was like to fuck me into the mattress?" Because Law did.

"I want your pants down. I want to lick you—fuck you—do things to you that'll make you walk funny for days," Styx told him in a voice husky with want that Law remembered well.

Neither had been a virgin when they'd met but Styx had more experience. And while Law had been reluctant to bottom, with Styx he turned submissive immediately, allowing Styx his ass after he'd been stripped down and kissed like there was no tomorrow.

Law could still hear his words of surrender to Styx, whispered on that cold winter's night a month after Styx moved into Greg's house… *Fuck me now, Styx…can't wait anymore.*

And Styx had done just that. Law had craved him in the old days and apparently, his dick still did because Law nearly reached under his body to unbutton and unzip his own jeans. But then Styx flipped him onto his back and pinned his arms under his knees, straddled him, his jean-clad cock bulging. Styx moved his hands behind him to do the honors of Law's jeans, freeing his cock, and Law cursed not wearing underwear tonight.

He'd figured none would be needed in his plans with

Paulo.

Paulo. Law bucked in an effort to shove Styx off him, even though he was completely torn about staying put.

"You didn't complain when I got you off at the restaurant. But go ahead, you know you like it better when you resist," Styx told him, and his voice was…gentle. Smooth.

"Don't," he begged hoarsely, although his dick was hard against Styx's hand, and he held his breath, not sure which decision Styx would make.

But it was Paulo who did so by coming in quietly and clearing his throat to get their attention. Law imagined they were quite a sight, with him mostly undressed and Styx sitting on him, and their intent must've been obvious.

But Paulo simply eyed the two bodies appreciatively and then said, "I wonder if you two are planning on acting your age—wouldn't want you old men hurting yourselves."

Fucking wiseass turned with a smirk and shut the door. Both Law and Styx could still hear him laughing, even as Styx rolled off Law and sat with his back against the wall.

"I'd put him over my knee," Styx said, and yeah, that would be something Law wouldn't mind watching, because it would be fodder for fantasy for a long time to come, even though he'd never tell Styx that.

Instead, he jerked away from Styx. "You don't put him anywhere—he's mine."

And then he got up off the floor and went into the next bedroom, determined to prove it.

4

Paulo had heard the fight over the TV and his hand had remained on the doorknob for a few long moments, trying to assess if Law needed him.

Sixteen years was a long time apart, and the CIA—hell, any law enforcement, government or military work—did things to a man. Styx might not be the same person Law thought he was.

And so he opened the door, had been standing there for longer than either Styx or Law knew before he'd cleared his throat to make his presence known. Couldn't help it, really—it was…hot. Fascinating. Incredible. The two big men grinding together like gladiators fighting it out to the death.

That's what this was—nothing more, nothing less than love. Paulo could see it in both men's eyes—their actions, while rough, were nothing short of a major turn-on for him because of the underlying tenderness.

Paulo watched Styx strip and get Law onto his back, telling Law, "Go ahead—you know you like it better when you resist"

The power and the struggle between the two men was simply an awesome display. Two gladiators, fighting to get their fill.

Paulo's mouth had gone dry as he watched them wrestle, all the while knowing how it would end, and yet he was unable to look away.

Watching Law with someone else could hurt him, but somehow, watching him with Styx was all right. Because this was a man who loved Law for real and Paulo understood that sentiment with a ferocity that scared him.

He'd held Law up as a jerk-off fantasy long before he'd ever had occasion to approach him. And Law was so much better than the fantasy, which rarely happened.

He'd been hard just thinking about it, but now his cock was impossibly so. It was going to happen right in front of him. The two powerful men rolled along the floor and Paulo knew it was only a matter of time before Law conceded. He'd loved the man for too long, and all the pent-up anger only fueled the already sexually tense situation.

And so Paulo moved away, because he didn't want to spy on them, not like this, because the fight would soon turn into an intimate moment.

But when he heard Styx mention the hand job, that pissed the hell out of him. He'd been worried about Law in the restaurant and Law had been too busy getting off to worry about anything else.

Motherfucker.

In his life, sometimes he'd fought for what he wanted—most times, he hadn't wanted anything that badly and so he'd simply walked away.

This time, he couldn't do that. The need for Law was simply too great.

This time, he would fight.

So yes, he'd known what he was doing when he'd goaded Law and Styx, but he hadn't thought Law would come at him like a charging bull.

Didn't think he'd kick the door closed behind him, yank off his already undone pants and come at Paulo with a fire in his eyes and a cock as hard as glass.

"Hands up," he ordered Paulo, and Paulo didn't bother to protest. Law stripped the T-shirt off him, used it to bind his wrists together and then to the headboard with a hard knot, then sucked hard on a nipple while cupping his cock through his jeans.

He'd still been aroused from their earlier kissing session so Law's hot mouth on his skin made his body jolt. He drew in a sharp, jerky breath and arched into Law, because he didn't want the man to stop sucking or fondling…needed the contact more intensely than he'd ever needed it before.

This was reassurance…this was everything.

Law scraped his teeth over the now taut nipple, tugged it between them, making Paulo cry out.

"More, Law," he managed, his voice close to breaking

because Law was doing it just right, like he was getting to the root of a pleasure spot few could hit.

But Law pulled back then, stared down at him.

"Old man?" Law's tone was dangerous, and Paulo swallowed hard, especially when Law yanked down his jeans and circled Paulo's cock with his hand. He stroked hard, and Paulo arched again, precome spilling. His balls tightened and he would have to force himself not to come all over his stomach immediately. "How about this old man fucking you until you can't walk?"

"You…can…try," Paulo managed, and the pent-up tension he'd noted in Law was going to spill over into him.

"How you under-fucking-estimate me," Law growled against his mouth before he got off and searched for lube, found it in the pocket of his jeans and came back with a thick smear of it on his two middle fingers and a condom on his already impossibly hard cock.

He nudged Paulo's thighs far apart as Paulo fought for the wiseass persona he'd had just minutes earlier, but once Law's fingers entered him, all bets were off. The fingers scissored and twisted together, taking his ass and making him rock to Law's rhythm while Law watched his face.

"Yeah, you like that, baby?"

He opened his mouth to respond but a moan came out instead, especially when Law hit his prostate with a knuckle and then held the base of Paulo's cock with his other hand so he couldn't come too soon.

"Did that turn you on to watch?" Law asked, and fuck yeah, it had. Was it not supposed to? Paulo could usually handle himself in any situation, but this one had him spinning.

"Yes," Paulo heard himself say, and Law replaced his fingers with his cock. When Law entered him, a long, hard stroke until Paulo called out—maybe it was Law's name or *more* or both because Law grinned, leaned back on his heels and held Paulo's hips, yanking him harder into his cock. Took him with a ferocity that made Paulo whimper with surrender, only too glad Law hadn't given him the choice.

He didn't want one. Watched Law's face as he pounded his ass, his prostate damned near singing from the constant contact, and it was almost too much, but he couldn't give in this fast. Couldn't give Law that complete satisfaction, because fuck it all, the man had been ready to let Styx take him.

Paulo shut his eyes for a second and imagined what that would've been like…if they'd have invited him inside had he walked in any later.

When he opened his eyes, a movement over Law's shoulder caught his eye. Styx, standing by the door, watching Paulo, and Paulo could imagine what Styx was seeing: Paulo with his wrists tied to the bedposts, spread, being thoroughly fucked.

He didn't leave and Paulo was incoherent, unable to tell Law or maybe Law knew and didn't care, because indeed, his only big concern at the moment seemed to be plowing Paulo. And maybe Styx had come in to reclaim Law, to punch Paulo for his earlier remarks…but the man didn't appear to be angry. Just the opposite—he was turned on, his eyes glazed with lust as Paulo felt them rake him.

What would it be like to have that man's hands on him? What would it be like to be in between them, in every sense?

When he looked up at Law again, he had a small grin tugging the corner of his mouth. He knew…and he knew it turned Law on.

"Go ahead and watch him watching you, baby, if that's turning you on."

Paulo looked at Styx again—the man was smiling. Had moved closer to the bed, his arousal unmistakable through his jeans…

"Gonna call me old again?" Law asked, and Paulo looked between him and Styx and shook his head. "Yeah, you will…and I'll just have to keep fucking you blind every time you so much as think it."

Styx nodded his assent and then their eyes locked as Paulo came, hard as he ever had, at the same time Law's orgasm ripped through him. His eyes shifted to Law, who smiled at him the way Paulo had wanted him to from day one, and somehow, he knew they'd all won in some small way tonight.

The pleasure seared him from head to toe, the throb of

his climax overtook every part of him, made him shudder and shake and fucking nearly lose consciousness, at least until he heard Law whispering his name against his cheek, holding him much more tenderly than he had before.

When Paulo finally opened his eyes again, Styx was long gone, but most definitely not forgotten by either man in the bed.

Law eased out of him slowly, but Paulo still winced. It had been a rough ride and he'd be feeling it for a while, and still his ass missed the contact of Law's dick. He watched Law head to the bathroom and when he came back, he had a washcloth that he used to clean Paulo.

Normally, Paulo didn't like to be fussed over like this, but he didn't protest since Law seemed intent on the task at hand.

When he was done, he threw the cloth in the general direction of the bathroom, untied Paulo and lay next to the younger man, propped on an elbow.

"Did he tell you what's going on?" Paulo asked finally, because that for sure was the safer of the topics right now, and God, what a fucking commentary on their situation that was.

"He did." Law told him everything about Styx's assassin father, the CIA's involvement, Styx's continued lack of memory…and the fact that Styx's father wouldn't back down this time.

When Law finished, Paulo closed his eyes and turned

over, letting the threat of danger settle over him like a heavy blanket.

What this meant for all of them was something Paulo knew could turn very serious. It wasn't only about Styx taking out his father—it was making sure he didn't bring retribution down on all their heads.

Paulo could only imagine how the conversation had turned into this intense thing he'd walked in on. All he said was, "You knew he was watching us."

"And you were watching him."

At the semi-accusation in Law's voice, Paulo turned back to him, asked, "Wait—you almost let him fuck you and then you came to me and now you're pissed at a... fantasy?"

He hadn't meant to say it quite like that, but it had slipped out and now he'd have to deal with the consequences.

"Is that what he is—part of your fantasy?" Law asked.

"Were you fucking me or him?"

"You, Paulo. But you knew that."

He did, but he also knew it was Styx who'd set Law's blood to boiling this time. Paulo had simply taken him the rest of the way.

And while Paulo had for sure enjoyed the ride, he was also confused as hell. "You didn't come around for three months."

"And then I did," Law said softly.

"Were you just bored? Horny?"

"Horny and bored would have me getting off in the clubs, and that hasn't been the same since you," Law admitted.

"Sorry to interfere with your casual fucking."

"You were celibate the whole time you didn't see me?"

Paulo remained silent because no, definitely not. He'd been desperate to get the feelings Law stirred in him gone… and it hadn't worked worth a damn.

"I didn't think so," Law said. And then, "Who was he? Or was there more than one?"

Paulo was enjoying Law's jealousy way more than he thought he would. "Didn't think you'd mind."

"I mind," Law growled, pulling Paulo against him and kissing him hard. "I fucking mind a lot."

"Your past is in the next room and it's nowhere near past. Am I supposed to not mind that?"

"I don't know, Paulo. Can we get through this situation and then figure it out?"

"If all the secrets are laid out, sure," Paulo said, but he didn't push further, and Law let go of the ominous feeling he always got when someone made an attempt to learn about his past.

"Hey, you're keeping secrets from me, too. Styx might've had you checked out, but I knew something was up," Law told him. "Is what he said true, about not staying in one place very long?"

"Yeah."

"Would you have left without telling me first?"

Paulo's gaze was steady, his voice firm even as he lied through his teeth. "No. Never."

Law let it slide. Before this, he hadn't probed into Paulo's past because he didn't like when anyone tried to talk about his. But Styx had obviously investigated Paulo…and if he hadn't liked what he'd found, Paulo would not be here with them.

Styx had found something that made him want Paulo with them, which could really only mean one thing.

Paulo was a lost boy, just like them. With that in mind, he pulled Paulo to him tightly, and Paulo let him, buried his face in Law's chest and for a long while they just lay there, letting everything sink in.

"Not how I pictured tonight," he mumbled, and Law chuckled.

"You weren't complaining earlier."

Paulo lifted his head sleepily. "Never complain about spending time with you, Law."

Law. Slowly, he was starting to think of himself that way as well. Despite—or maybe because of the danger, he hadn't felt this alive forever. "Did you really hang around longer than you would have…because of me?"

"Why do you sound like that's so hard to believe?" Paulo asked. "I waited my whole life to feel about someone the way I feel about you. Patience was all I had in the end."

"While you waited for me to come to my senses, right?"

"Something like that."

"I guess we've both got secrets."

"You want to know mine?" Paulo asked. "I was about to put in my notice at the precinct. Because of this, it sounds like I will, anyway. But it was time to move on."

"I guess you have your reasons...but in light of what's happened, I need to know if someone's looking for you."

"It's nothing like that. Styx didn't spill the details?"

"No, and I didn't ask him."

"But suddenly, you want to know things. You're all interested. I guess I should've saved your life earlier."

Law sighed. "Yeah, all right, that's fair. I pushed you away for a long time. I've been an asshole—you knew that about me from before we met."

"Yeah, I did. I guess that's what drew me to you in the first place." Paulo's words dripped with sarcasm.

"That and my boots," Law said, reminding Paulo of the fantasy the younger man told him on their first date, a fantasy he'd had in the months leading up to actually meeting Law at Crave. And that made Paulo smile a little, letting it tug the corner of his mouth up.

"Is that why you wore them tonight?" Paulo asked, glanced over to the corner where Law had shed them before he'd come at Paulo like a tornado.

"I'll do anything that turns you on."

Paulo shook his head as he considered that. After a few long moments, he started to talk about the story Styx had alluded to. "My father's an ex-New York City cop—he was jailed on a corruption charge about ten years ago. It was a big deal—hit all the national papers. He was abusing prisoners. He and his partner went too far and they couldn't cover it up. The hospital got suspicious and they were brought up on charges. My father's defense was that the guy was gay—that he propositioned them…they said the prisoner abused himself in order to frame the cops."

"Did he know you're gay?"

"He knew. Keeping it a secret from my family was never an option for me. It would be like cutting off an arm and trying to live. I never came out at work—I understood the dangers inherent in that. But my father was disgusted. He said, *everyone's going to know by looking at you.*"

"Yeah, the scarlet G you have burned onto your forehead," Law muttered.

"I was on the force maybe eight months when it broke. I had to get the hell out of there before he was convicted, even though his lawyers tried to persuade me to stay through the trial. I was getting death threats. People thought I was like him. They figured, like father, like son…a bigoted bastard." Paulo shook his head. "It's the ultimate irony."

"I'm sorry, Paulo."

"I started moving around, precinct to precinct. Someone always brings it up eventually. Then it spreads through the department and people figure I'm just like him. Even my sergeants get suspicious. How the fuck am I supposed to work like that?" Paulo's eyes were hot with anger. "It's gotten so bad, I'm going to have to go private. I planned on it after this stint in North Carolina."

Law nodded. "Do you talk to your father at all?"

"No. He's out now—did six years because he pleaded to a lesser charge. I don't talk to anyone in my family. They're pissed at me for leaving the city, for being gay…it's easier to be on my own."

"Sounds lonely."

"Nothing's perfect."

Law thought about Paulo drifting from place to place, never forming any ties. Always worried his past would come out. "You deserve better."

Paulo kicked out from the sheets and sat up, his back to Law. He stayed there a long time and then he finally said, "I know what I deserve and what I want. But what do you see in me? Besides the tattoos."

Goddamn, Law loved those. His dick hardened just at the mention, which made him stare again at Paulo's back and arms, and he got up and sat next to Paulo. "You make me nervous. That hasn't happened in forever. The only other person I've ever said that to was Styx."

He guessed that Greg had been wrong—lightning did indeed strike twice. Now, Law just needed to figure out what to do with it.

"Control's all I ever had," Law continued. "Giving it up in any situation—including during sex—is hard for me."

"Did you lose it with me?"

"You couldn't tell?" Law asked softly. "Jesus, Paulo, I don't go on dates…or spend the night. I'm all about anonymous sex, no strings, no talk of personal life. And with you, I couldn't keep that shield up. Couldn't not see you, and for a while, I hated you because I wanted you. And then I couldn't stay away."

Law's confession made Paulo's chest ache, especially when he thought about how close he'd come to putting in his resignation at the precinct. It was written, printed out, sitting on his desk, and every day Paulo would pick it up, think about folding it up into the envelope sitting next to it and bringing it into the precinct with him.

The only thing he knew for sure was that his next move wouldn't be to another precinct. No it would be to something he could do on his own—PI or bounty hunting or bail bonding…anything where he couldn't be found out by a group of coworkers.

But staying close to Law—without him—would be too hard.

"What're you thinking?"

"I thought I'd lost you…in the restaurant, when I heard the shot…" Paulo trailed off and Law buried his head against his shoulder.

"Me too. Fuck."

"Bastard," Paulo blurted out. "I was worried, and you were getting off."

Law didn't deny it, and Paulo figured that his honesty in this case could only help things.

"So, is this stuff with Styx going to be about exorcizing your ghosts?" Paulo asked.

"Maybe. Or maybe it's about beginnings." Law paused. "The Law/LC thing—for a long time, I couldn't think of myself as Law. The memories it brought back, not just of Styx, but of Damon…what happened to him when we were younger."

Paulo knew. A few months earlier, Law had been hurt by an attacker outside Crave who turned out to be someone from Damon and Law's past, the man responsible for Damon's gang rape at eighteen.

Law had already told him he felt completely responsible for what had happened, reiterated it now. "If I'd gone out with Damon…"

"Are you ever going to realize you can't blame yourself for that? For anything that happened that night, especially Styx leaving?" Paulo shifted. "Why he did, that's his thing. He did it to protect you."

"Now you're on his side?"

Law looked angry, but fuck it. Paulo was more so—he simply hid it better. "I'm on your side, Law. I've always been. And you've never been anything but completely honest with me. I'm not going to be the one who holds you back from Styx. You'd never forgive me for that—and I'd never have a shot in hell."

"You're not holding me back—I can make my own decisions. I'm in here with you, right?"

"We weren't alone in here tonight. We're still not. And the weird part is…I can understand. You alone…you rocked me, and I never thought that would happen. But you with Styx…"

Law smiled because he understood. "He's something. Hard to resist. Always was."

"You shouldn't be. The bond between you—it's physical, but it's the way he treats you. He still goddamn loves you. Maybe that's what makes it easier for me to defend him to you. I want to hate him, but I can't."

Law didn't bother arguing with anything he said. "I think he feels the same way about you."

"He thinks I'm an asshole."

"He said you needed a spanking. I'm inclined to agree with him that you're overdue," Law said. For the first time since this started, Paulo felt cornered, and his dick told him he liked it.

"I thought you weren't into all that BDSM shit," Paulo said, well aware his voice sounded raw.

Law noticed. "Some of it's useful. I've picked up some stuff living with a Dom all these years."

Paulo wasn't ready for this—for any of it—and he drew

in a deep breath when the dizziness started. Was he having a panic attack?

He vaguely heard Law telling him to fucking breathe, was aware that Styx was there too, pushing his head between his legs until he felt better. Murmuring against his ear to just breathe, and even though he hadn't known Styx long at all, he'd already come to associate the smell of peppermint with him. He stayed there for a while, with both men's hands on his back and neck, rubbing, encouraging. He felt the drag of a wet washcloth on his skin, remembered he was still naked, elbows on his knees, head hanging and his dick half hard despite his nearly passing out.

Law and Styx sat so close to him, and he let that comfort him…which it strangely did. He could tell their touches apart, even though both men were gentle.

When he finally sat up straight, he felt like a fucking wimpy asshole, but neither man looked at him like that.

"I'm okay. Thanks." He looked at Law and then Styx and realized that both were still touching him, Law with a hand on his thigh and Styx with the washcloth on the back of his neck.

Styx's eyes traveled over his body and Paulo felt the blush rise in his cheeks. Hoped it was hidden by the flush covering his body from the goddamned panic attack. And when he met Styx's eyes, he saw approval there…and he didn't know why that was so fucking important, but it was.

"When's the last time you ate?" Styx asked.

"I didn't." Paulo remembered the wine and a few appetizers at the restaurant and no lunch before that.

"I'll go get him something." Styx stood and handed Law a gun he took out of the back of his jeans. "Do you remember how to use that?"

"Fuck you," Law told him, took the gun and watched Styx leave before turning back to Paulo. "I didn't mean to push you."

"Yeah, you did." Paulo sank back into the bed. "And I never said I didn't like it."

Law didn't know what to say to that, to anything that was happening, and so he pulled the covers up over Paulo's naked body. He didn't understand the electric current running between the three of them, chalked it up to danger and stress—because fucking was another form of adrenaline rush relief.

But there was something more there he wasn't ready to unravel. Not tonight, anyway. "Sleep, man."

Paulo nodded, muttered, "Don't think I'll be able to," and then passed out as the last word was spoken. That made Law smile, and he rubbed the back of Paulo's neck for a few minutes, watching him sleep.

About ten minutes later, Styx came in quietly, put the fast food bags on the table. "It's the only thing open and close by."

"He's asleep."

Styx looked over at Paulo, peacefully curled in the blankets. "You should wake him—make him eat something. We can't risk him getting sick."

"I told him…about you."

Styx's jaw clenched, and he nodded. "I suppose you had no choice."

"That's about the only thing I have no choice in."

"Not going there right now."

"Did you like what you saw?"

"Yeah, I did," Styx shot back. "I didn't hear either of you ask me to leave."

That was true. Knowing Styx was there, witnessing everything, made the entire experience off the charts when Law should've been pissed as hell.

"I was a part of it, whether I was there or not," Styx added.

"That's basically what Paulo said." Law sat at the small table and Styx passed him a burger and fries before taking his own and sitting across from him. For a while, they ate in silence, taking in the enormity of all the situations.

Finally, Law crumpled the paper from his burger and looked at Styx. "Any action outside?"

"All quiet."

"That's good." He paused. "Can I ask you something?"

Styx just nodded with a world-weary look on his face

that brought Law back to the first weeks they'd known each other—it was Styx's universal look for, "You can ask and I'm sure it's going to bug the shit out of me."

Law didn't care. "What's your real name?"

His former lover's face hardened and when he spoke, it was with an uncouched fierceness. "It's Styx. That's the one I chose—the only one I answer to."

Law accepted that because a piece of paper with a name on it was just that. The fact that Styx had been forced back into that violence turned his stomach, so badly that he needed an outlet for the pain and anger.

How anyone could fuck up their kids so badly... Shit, why bother having them at all?

He knew Styx was good at his job with the CIA—knew what he'd been trained to do. Law, as a Delta, had learned to kill quickly and efficiently when necessary. The world of Special Ops and the alphabet agencies that surrounded them was full of men with murky pasts, shady presents and uncertain futures. Sometimes, it was too easy to fall into the trap of thinking you were the job.

Had that happened to Styx? He appeared the same—he'd always been serious and sarcastic but had always been able to drag Law out of his shell.

"When your father was in prison, did you ever see him or talk to him?"

Styx shook his head. "I knew what I needed to. He wouldn't have given a reason why because it was what he did…who he was. The fact that I didn't turn out exactly like him… Well, there wouldn't have been any love if I had."

That was true but it didn't make it any easier to deal with. "I'm sorry."

"Not your fault."

"I wish I could've been there for you. I wanted to."

"I didn't want you involved in that. I still don't."

"Case you haven't noticed, I'm a big boy."

Styx didn't relent. "I don't care—and this is my decision."

So how could any kind of relationship grow under these circumstances? How had they?

Because they'd been young…clinging to each other.

But Law hadn't been waiting for Styx for nothing…no, the man was the same underneath it all, and probably a lot more like Paulo than either man cared to admit, and that intrigued Law a hell of a lot.

Styx stood then. "I'll let you grab some shut-eye."

Both Law and Styx glanced over at Paulo, who was still out like a light.

"Sleeps like a baby."

Law cocked a brow. "The only time I'd compare him to one. Otherwise…"

Styx let his eyes linger on the younger man. "Does he heal you?"

"He's trying," Law admitted as Styx turned his gaze back to him. "I was already halfway there with you."

5

Sleep had always been a joke, but there had been next to none for Styx that night. He'd left Law and Paulo's room with Law's words still echoing in his brain, closed the door between the rooms and jerked off in the shower quickly, the threat of danger never really leaving his mind.

He had no doubt the two men realized their lives were in jeopardy, but the complete and utter horror of the entire situation hadn't hit home for them yet.

Styx had no doubt his father—or his father's henchmen— had already ripped through Law's apartment and Paulo's as well. Their lives would never be the same unless he could eradicate his father and the group of men who worked under him.

Thus far, that had proved to be impossible. And so he remained on the bed, alone, coming up with several plans to present to Tomcat, because this could go so many different ways.

With all of them, Law would hate him, because it meant leaving again.

When the sun came up, Tomcat texted him that the safe house was all set, that he'd meet them there with the necessary supplies and to haul ass before the storm came. That a truck had been dropped off in the back lot for him, which Styx already had a key to.

March snow wasn't unheard of in upstate New York, which was where they were now headed, but this had been one of the worst winters on record. So he knocked on the door and got Law and Paulo moving. Styx pulled the truck around for them and they picked up breakfast along the way.

All in all, it was an eight-hour drive that was mostly silent. Paulo crawled into the back to sleep, leaving Styx to wonder if Law had fucked him all night or if he'd slept through.

He'd bet sleep, though, because from what he'd witnessed, Paulo wasn't quiet and damn, it had been something… and he should be jealous but he wasn't, not really, and he wondered why.

He was intrigued by Paulo, by Law's reaction to him and by his own.

But by the morning, the lust had dissipated and the heavy cloak of reality shrouded everything. This wasn't about a single night of confessions and fights and sex… This had implications that could last each of them a lifetime, and the blame weighed on Styx heavily.

"We're here," Styx said quietly, and Law shook Paulo

awake. He parked next to Tomcat's truck and the men all got out and stretched.

"All clear?" Styx asked Tomcat, who nodded. Styx handed Law the keys and he and Paulo headed inside while Styx waited to talk with his partner.

In his truck, the man had clothes for all the men, plus food and other supplies, like gas for the truck and the generator. And shovels, because the snow was expected to come down like a motherfucker, land-locking them here for a couple of days. It would ensure no one could get to them…although Styx still had his doubts about that.

Tomcat caught a look at Styx's bruised cheek, courtesy of Law last night. "Looks like you told him everything."

Styx ignored him in favor of unpacking the boxes from the back.

They'd used this place before, but Styx had always been the one dropping people off here, and although he welcomed the time with Law, these weren't the most ideal circumstances.

"They broke into Paulo's apartment. Law's too but not Damon's," Tomcat confirmed when Styx returned from his second trip into the house.

Styx cursed and punched the hood of the truck lightly a few times with the side of his closed fist.

"I checked the intel on Damon—he's away for two weeks with Tanner James," Tomcat continued.

The only bright spot in all of this. Law had mentioned

their trip to Europe and Styx had asked Tomcat to run it, just to be sure.

"The cop's good," Tomcat said, and Styx narrowed his eyes. Because Tomcat never complimented anyone—and not like that. Especially not cops. "What? I'm stating a truth."

"Forget it," he muttered, didn't want Paulo to be good at anything, but he was. Most obviously, he was good at making Law happy and how could Styx bitch about that? It was what he'd always wanted—Law to be happy.

"Hey, it could be a lot worse you were stuck with—you've got a detective and an ex-Delta."

Styx just shook his head. "It's a fucking nightmare."

"For some men, maybe. But you've got two men and nothing to do but—"

"Not get killed?"

"You know I get the seriousness of the sitch, man, but you've been mooning over Law for a hell of a long time."

"Helluva way to win him back."

"How do you know you ever lost him?"

"You met Paulo, right? The good one?"

Tomcat shrugged. "Law looks like he can handle an angel and a devil."

"You're impossible."

"We're going to catch the fucker." Tomcat could turn fierce in the space of an instant, and Styx knew his partner always had his back.

"I wish I could be as sure as you."

"Happened once. No one's that good for that long."

"I want you to be right."

"Take the next forty-eight to get your shit together. We'll work the rest out after that."

Tomcat was right. Leaving Law again right now would be stupid as hell. Styx knew he was literally down to his last chance and he'd be damned if he fucked it all up again.

"You're safe here for now," Tomcat said. "Besides, you said you wanted to take care of this part personally, let your friend know his options. Do that and then come back and we'll get the bastard."

Tomcat was right, reminded him as to why they'd tailed Law to the restaurant to begin with. Why Styx had spent the morning waiting for Law to exit Paulo's wearing the same clothing as the night before, slightly askew.

When he'd first met Tomcat, Styx knew him as Clint. Clint Sommers, who was a year older than Styx was and who'd gotten into the CIA because they'd taken note of his computer hacking abilities. Turned out, he was also damned good at playing secret agent and especially undercover work. Despite his height, he could camouflage himself into just about any role—his current one as part of a motorcycle gang necessitated the name Tomcat, and he'd spend over a year undercover. But he refused to stop helping Styx once his father escaped, and so now he was working both jobs simultaneously.

Disappearing from a motorcycle gang here and there wasn't too much of an issue, so he was lucky.

"I'm glad you're in on this," Styx told him now.

"Wouldn't have it any other way."

After Tomcat helped him bring in the last of the boxes, Styx walked him out and watched his truck take off—he wouldn't go too far—someplace he could get a chopper to help Styx if need be. And then he stayed outside for a while, needing the space from the situation—wanted the fresh air to clear his head, to figure out what the hell he was going to present as options to the two men inside. After Tomcat's truck disappeared, he walked the perimeter of the house, checking things out, and then spent a few minutes looking up at the gray sky.

But the memories were coming back to him too fast out here—worse than they had last night and all the nights before these past three months since he'd actually laid eyes on Law again.

Having no memories before the age of sixteen was frightening—a big, black hole he couldn't dwell on without freaking out. And not much freaked him out. Being in the CIA since he'd turned himself in at twenty-one had really sucked most of that out of him.

But those first moments of remembering were like being born again—painful and necessary.

He'd been sixteen years old, and he'd woken up on a Central Park bench with blood on his shirt. Not a lot and it wasn't his, but he shed it immediately, sat there and panicked because he didn't know what the hell to do next. Didn't know who he was, where he'd come from, and so he walked a few blocks bare-chested, despite the cold temperatures. Met up with a guy who wanted to party with him and ended up in Greg's club purely by happenstance.

According to Greg, nothing was ever coincidence—it was all fate, and Styx had wanted to call that theory crap but he couldn't.

Greg had brought him home—he'd wondered if something weird was going to happen, but he'd been too tired and scared to care. He'd showered and slept and no one bothered him—and when he woke, he stumbled on Law.

Jesus, that boy, nearly a man like Styx, hovering on that precipice, took his breath away. Blond, blue eyes, a wary, who-the-fuck-are-you look in his eyes.

Definitely love at first sight for him. For Law, too, even though it took the bastard a while to admit it.

He felt as nervous as he did that morning but he refused to put it off any longer—went back inside and began to unpack the boxes, dealing with the food first.

The house had three bedrooms and baths upstairs. Downstairs housed an eat-in kitchen and a good-sized living room and smaller den, all furnished courtesy of the CIA and actually better than most. But it wouldn't be big enough for the three of them—he wasn't sure any place would be big enough for that dynamic.

He shoved the last of the food in the fridge and turned to see Law and Paulo standing there. They'd been in the living room for a while, probably talking about what to say to him, as evidenced by the way Paulo started in immediately.

"How long are we here for?" he asked.

"A few days—through the snow." He dug into his pocket and handed Paulo a throwaway phone Tomcat had packed, as promised. "Call your boss, get the time off. Don't tell them what's happening."

Paulo nodded, took the phone and went into the next room while Styx continued to unpack. "There are clothes here for all of us. Sneakers and boots, too."

Law didn't say anything, continued to watch him carefully, but the wary truce from the night before was giving way.

Styx tried to ward it off at the pass. "What do you want me to say, man? I'm sorry. I'm sorry as hell—I stayed away for what seemed like forever to avoid this, Law. If I could take it back, I would." Dammit, his voice broke and he turned away.

"What's the plan? Tell us about witness protection and then you run free, trying to take down your father? Because that's bullshit and it'll just keep you running, the same way you've been. You'll just be going in a different direction," Law told him.

He should've known Law would be a step ahead of

him—and completely fucking right. "It's the best thing for you and Paulo."

"Fuck you and your knowing what's best for us," Law spat.

"Cut him a break, Law."

Paulo's voice. He'd obviously caught most of the conversation, tossed Styx back the phone with a nod before Law turned to Paulo. "You know nothing about this."

"I'm here, aren't I? And I've got a pretty good idea about what's happening between you two." Paulo's eyes flashed. "He cares about you, and you've gotten really good at pushing people who care about you away."

"Now you're on his side?"

"It's not his fault. Not really."

Law sagged against the fridge, ran his hands through his hair. "Dammit, you don't know."

"I know you two have a connection. I know you grew up together. I know a hell of a lot more than you think."

At Paulo's words, Law stiffened, and Styx realized that the real battle had just begun.

Paulo couldn't stand to watch the two men rip each other to shreds, not when they'd just ended up together again after all these years.

Styx was Law's first love. After everything Paulo had

discovered about Law, he knew that the man deserved all the happiness in the world.

"What the fuck are you talking about?" Law asked, his voice dangerous, but Paulo never let that shit get to him. It might turn him on, but intimidate him? No goddamned way.

He started again, "After all you've been through…" but Law interrupted him abruptly.

"You're not just talking about what happened at Crave, are you?"

Put-up or shut-up time. "No, I'm not. I know. About you."

"What do you mean, you know?"

"Your medical records…from when you were younger." Paulo glanced at Styx, whose expression had gone hard again and he wondered if both men were going to attempt to kick his ass for this.

"Aren't there laws that keep you from invading my personal medical history—my CPS records?" Law demanded, and yes, Paulo had bypassed those quite nicely.

Yeah, this was bad. All he could do was nod.

"And you thought my past was your business?" Law continued.

"I still do."

"Dammit, Paulo." Law turned, stayed with his back to both him and Styx for a very long while and time was suspended, their relationship—what little there had been—hanging in the balance. The tension was palpable. But Paulo had always known he'd be the one to bring this up with Law. Law would never be the one to tell him that information, no matter how long they'd stay together.

"I'm sorry. I wanted you to tell me…but I knew you wouldn't," Paulo said finally.

"Right, because it was fucking private," Law spat.

"I'm tired of secrets," Paulo said. "I'm tired of keeping them—of having them kept from me."

"So this is payback? Because you had this information long before I asked you about your past last night."

"No, it's about getting the goddamned truth out. I have to be able to trust both of you if my ass is on the line. I need to know every fucking thing."

Styx was watching both of them quietly. He'd have to be a fool to get in the middle of this, and if Paulo learned anything after twenty-four hours with the man, he knew Styx was anything but.

Still, Paulo was surprised Styx didn't grab him by the throat for pissing Law off, for spilling his private life out like that.

Then again, Styx was surprising Paulo in a lot of ways.

"You—" Law pointed to Paulo, "—and you." This time, his attention turned to Styx. "Both of you and your secrets can go fuck yourselves. I'm done with this."

"You can't just walk out," Paulo said.

"Watch me." Law turned then, grabbed one of the guns

off the kitchen table and left the house, slamming out the front door.

It was more to prove his point—he wasn't going far in this storm, but still, "Get him," Paulo told Styx.

"He's too pissed." Styx stared out the window, watching Law walk toward the back of the house. "Besides, we're in the middle of bumblefuck—it's one of the benefits."

Paulo walked into the living room, slumped onto the couch, and Styx moved to the kitchen doorway. "I shouldn't have pried into his records. Are you going to tell me what an asshole I am?"

Styx's next words surprised the hell out of him. "No. Because I did the same thing."

6

Law couldn't remember being more fucking furious with someone since…fuck, since Styx and his nosing around. Goddammit, the two assholes inside were perfect for one another. And they were welcome to each other, because Law didn't want either of them.

Although that was a big fucking lie. He sat on the stone wall that ran the entire length of the back of the house and faced the woods, letting the first flakes of the storm float past him.

He'd always loved the snow—everything was quiet and calm and he could think. But today there would be too much time to do so, and his bones ached in anticipation of the storm.

He rubbed his arms, grateful that Styx had shoved some Advil at him first thing that morning. A sign that the man remembered everything.

Paulo had done the same for him when he'd stayed at his apartment two nights before.

Paulo…dammit.

If Paulo had read his records, he really did know everything, and Law could no longer pretend that it didn't happen.

Fuck, if Paulo looked at him with pity…

But he hadn't, ever. And Law had radar for that, was pretty bullshit-proof.

He wiped his eyes with the back of his hand and then rubbed them together, the cold not helping the deep ache.

He really had nearly every major bone in his body broken by the time he was ten—some more than once, and hell, he could predict rain and snow with an accuracy no meteorologist seemed to have.

It was gonna storm tonight.

Who was he kidding? It had already started, a long time ago when his father started drinking and his mother stopped giving a shit. Or maybe she never really had, but time had a way of fuzzing things over.

He remembered rarely having new clothes or books or anything—he and his brother had been taken from his parents twice only to find themselves in far worse situations where they didn't know the groundwork, the triggers.

It was in childhood when he'd learned the importance of stealth and recon, knew that when the bottles came out and the voices got louder, it was time to become invisible.

He'd been an easy target for a long time.

The physical abuse had been well documented for both Law and his brother, teachers noticing it from first grade on. The boys had been pulled from the house twice before the family moved from Connecticut to New York, and then they were in a much larger school system. They'd also learned to lie, because it was easier on them if no one suspected the truth.

But hospital records always noted the abuse—the social workers were always called down, spoke to Law in a sympathetic you-can-tell-me-everything tone and Law never did.

Over the years, that had become so ingrained in him that the thought of talking about any of it made him freeze up. He'd been pissed as hell that Greg had even mentioned it to Styx—and Damon, too—but then he'd been grateful he didn't have to do so himself.

Paulo wouldn't know everything, though. Because the most horrific part wasn't in the files. It was still an open crime and Paulo hadn't looked hard enough—or hadn't thought to look into the police files.

Law's brother had been missing for years. Although Law's father and mother had been questioned in his disappearance, since Law had also run away, they'd put the case down as unsolved.

Unsolved. Law's stomach clenched when he thought about it, because he could easily walk into the police station and solve it, but what good would it do any of them?

His parents were both dead—murdered, actually, and his brother had been murdered as well, the day Law left home for good.

He'd been fifteen and had just witnessed his father kill his older brother. Jason had only been ten months older, smaller than Law—and although he hadn't liked the fact that Law was gay he was still fiercely protective, always stepping in the way and trying to take the brunt of the beatings.

It usually resulted in both Jason and Law with bones broken. But that night, it had been so much more—a broken neck from a hard push down a small flight of stairs leading to the basement.

When his father left to hide the body and his mother had ordered him to shut his mouth and get into his room, Law did. He'd already been packed so he grabbed his bag and went out the window and headed to the club where he'd been working, washing glasses and cleaning up after school for the past three months.

Greg had taken one look at him and pointed to the cot in the back room. "Not very comfortable, but it'll be okay for a couple of nights."

"Gonna be longer than that. Can't go back."

"Why?"

All it took was that simple word and he told Greg everything. Greg's eyes got wet but he didn't cry and instead, he let Law do so.

To this day, Greg was the only person Law had ever told the full story to. Greg hadn't said a word about going to the police, had simply asked, "Will he come looking for you?"

"Not here. Can't go back to school either, or he'll have to answer for what happened to my brother. And they'll ask me." He'd loved his brother, although they'd never been close. Most of the time, they'd been pitted against one another for survival.

But to watch his father make good on his threat…

"Don't go there, Law. Nothing you could've done," Greg told him and from there, Law stayed and worked with Greg. At first, it was in the back room and then he'd go to Greg's for dinner and schooling, and then he'd moved into the second floor of Greg's brownstone, with Greg living on the third floor.

It had never been weird or wrong—Greg hadn't ever made an inappropriate move.

Greg had saved his life, later told him he did so because someone had once saved his in the same manner.

And then Damon and Styx moved in and Greg made them all get their GEDs and taught them club management. Taught them to be responsible gay men.

God, Law still had so much to learn. He looked up at the sky and let the snow skim his face. When he was in Delta, he would sometimes sit for hours, stock still, waiting for a target. Now, because of Styx, he was one again.

Styx would be the one to come get him soon. Law could feel him in his bones, the way he could sense the storm, and he wondered what went on between the two men inside the house.

He wanted to punch Styx, for no other reason than he and Paulo were bonding. Styx had Paulo sticking up for him now—what the hell was that?

But he knew…Styx was a force as powerful as anything he'd ever known. A raging ocean, a fierce thunderstorm… and still, there was a gentleness inside the man that called to Law like a siren song.

He could still remember the first time he'd met Styx. It was like two lost souls recognizing one another—the feeling more intense even than meeting Damon.

It still hadn't stopped him from being wary.

Although he trusted Greg's instincts, after the addition of this boy—man, he had to admit, because Styx had never been a boy—Law kept his distance.

He'd named himself Styx because he'd been going through Greg's collection of albums and Styx's Paradise Theater album caught his eye.

"You realize you're naming yourself after a river in hell," Greg had said, and Styx nodded with that gleam in his eye, and for the first time in the week he'd been in Greg's house, he'd smiled.

From where he'd been in the hallway watching, Law had smiled too.

Paulo stared at Styx, surprised as shit that the man wasn't pissed at him, and his heart definitely opened more for the man he'd been sure he would continue to hate for what he'd done to Law. Maybe they had more in common than Paulo could've imagined. "You broke into Law's records?"

"Not exactly. Not at first. I asked Greg about it and he finally told me a little bit about how Law came to him. From there, I did some research. When I confronted him, Law didn't speak to me for a week, but we were a lot younger then."

"Why did you do it?"

Styx shrugged. "Same reason you did. I was in love with him and I knew whatever happened was holding him back. I've known him since we were sixteen. He knew I couldn't remember. When I first asked him why he was there, he just said something about having a rough time at home." Styx gave a short bark of a laugh. "Can you imagine? A rough time at home. And then, when he started speaking to me again, he told me everything. He's had years to pretend none of it happened."

But it had, in such sick and sadistic ways that Paulo had thrown up halfway through reading the file and again when he'd finished. "How can you be so calm about it?"

"Calm?" Styx's eyes were an icy glitter in the now darkening room. "You don't even know half the story— it's not in the CPS files. But I know *everything*. I found his father ten years ago and I killed the bastard. His mother was already dead or I would've strangled her with my bare hands, woman or not. People like that don't deserve children." Styx took a step toward the couch. "Are you going to tell me I was wrong to do it? That I should've let the police handle it? Want to turn me in?"

"No." Paulo felt his hands shake. "I looked them up because I was ready to…" He paused. "I was ready to kill them…but they were already dead."

Styx nodded, a sudden, unbreakable bond occurring between the two men.

"Does he know what you did?" Paulo asked.

Styx shrugged. "He's never asked and I've never said."

"What else is there? What don't I know?" He'd suspected that Law's run to Greg's house hadn't been smooth.

"It would've been in the police records—you didn't push hard enough, but I suspect you couldn't bring yourself to read any more," Styx said with a quiet understanding. "But that's his story to tell now. We've done enough damage with this."

Paulo agreed. "I need to talk to him."

He didn't want Law to run, but Paulo understood that better than anyone. He'd been it for years. Now, sometimes he thought it was the only way he knew how to live… And what did that mean that he'd hung around for three months longer than he'd intended because the thought of leaving Law made him physically ill?

"There's something about Law," Paulo said. "It makes me

want to protect him."

"And fuck him at the same time," Styx finished.

"I was going to say, get fucked by him, but yeah, that's the general idea. Dammit, I'm all fucked up. Things were fine until I met him and now I'm all turned around."

"Law tends to do that to people. He did it to me the first time I saw him."

"And then what?"

"And then he pushed me away as hard as he could for months."

"What'd you do?"

"Pushed back, just like you. So let me go get him. He's already more pissed at me than you, anyway." Styx didn't move, though. "I know you love him. I saw you—in the hospital with him."

Paulo stared at him. "You were there?"

"He didn't know because I didn't go to him."

"Because I did?"

"Because it looked like you cared…and he looked at you like…fuck, he used to look at me like that."

"He still does."

As much as Styx wanted to believe Paulo, he couldn't let himself. "Too much time has passed…"

"No, it hasn't."

Styx shook his head. This wasn't going to work. "I'm going to make sure you and Law are safe—and then I'll take off."

"He won't let you."

"He won't have a choice."

"Sounds like you've never given him one."

"You know nothing about it, cop."

Paulo smiled as if he knew he'd twisted the knife deep. Paulo wasn't afraid of him on any level, wasn't intimidated, looked him straight in the eye. He could handle anything, including and especially Law, which made him more special than anything.

"We're just as screwed as you are—maybe even more so," Paulo said finally.

It was the truth.

"I'll bring him out of hiding," Styx said. "I'm the best bait there is."

It would be putting his life on the line but it was possibly the only way to keep Law and Paulo safe. Or maybe not… but he didn't know what else to do, short of going rogue, hunting down and killing the man himself, which was the other option he'd already considered. But once Tomcat got involved, the CIA was watching him too closely.

"I should've had him killed when he was in prison," Styx muttered.

"But you didn't. And you and I both know that he'll go after me and Law before he touches you. He wants you back, and it sounds like he'll go to any length to make that happen. So use me as bait instead."

"No."

"Why not? You've got nothing invested in me."

"Law does." With that, he left Paulo and went out in the snow, the wind buffeting around him, the night beginning to settle in.

Law was sitting on the stone wall that spanned the entire back of the property, facing the woods across the street. Was staring daggers at Styx as he walked toward him.

When Styx got close, he leaned against the wall next to Law. "You're taking your anger for me out on Paulo."

"I've got plenty to go around," Law told him through gritted teeth.

"Law, come on." Styx put a hand on his shoulder, which promptly got shoved off. Law jumped down from the wall, and the physical fight from last night was nowhere near done. It had simply been put on hold, and now Styx braced himself for Law's wrath.

"You need to back the hell off, go back inside and stay away from me," Law told him, with fists clenched at his side.

"Or else?"

"I'm going to kick your ass, Styx."

"You and what army?" The words were a flashback to Greg's, when Styx, who'd been trying to get Law to talk to him, had pushed too far. They'd fought it out, a blend of testosterone and fear making it that much more potent.

Styx wasn't sure which of them won the battle that day, but he was pretty confident in the fact that he'd won the war, because he'd gotten Law into bed. Somewhere between the punches there were kisses that tasted like mint and strokes, and then he'd had Law's clothes off, was pressing him to the bed…

"I know what you're thinking about." Law's voice brought him back to the present. "You can forget that happening."

"I don't want to fight with you."

"But I do. I need to finish what we started last night—but only the fight part." Law came at him as the snow fell harder, fat flakes clinging to their clothes and the ground, and Styx tried to subdue him, get him to the point where the fight would leave him.

Because Law wasn't fighting him—he was fighting his past—and the helplessness and the fear that it had churned up inside of him. The regret that he'd stayed too long at his parents' house instead of escaping with his brother was a pain that never went away for him. And so Styx took the place of all those ghosts, let Law wear himself out until the man sagged against him, face buried in Styx's chest as silent tears fell.

They stood there, Styx holding Law up for he didn't know how long until Law all too characteristically pushed him away.

"Don't." Law pointed at him.

"I was comforting you—that's allowed, you know. You

can break down every once in a while."

Law's eyes were wet, but they still glittered with anger. "You don't know me anymore—stop acting like you know me so well."

"But I do."

Law was about to come at him again, but he turned instead, paced a little in front of the old stone wall, muttering to himself.

"Come inside, talk to him," Styx urged. "You can't go anywhere in this weather anyway, and it's too fucking cold out here."

"I have nothing to say to him. To you."

"You have everything to say to him. You know that as well as I do."

7

Paulo leaned back into the couch cushions and cursed himself silently. It was true, what he'd told Styx earlier—Law certainly didn't need to be protected, but that was all Paulo wanted to do.

Styx was as protective of Law as Paulo was. He understood everything—and really, he should've been Paulo's greatest adversary. Instead, the man was on his side, leaving Paulo confused as hell.

What the fuck was it about Law that had twisted him inside out from the second he'd laid eyes on the man?

The sex, for sure. Law knew his way around a man's body and had this way of focusing on you like you were the only goddamned person that ever existed in the world. Which was why the man pretty much had him at the first kiss.

Paulo didn't know if Law was like that with everyone and didn't really want to think about it, but Law made him feel like he mattered, like every touch and lick and suck was all about Paulo...like nothing mattered but keeping him happy.

Law's focus in bed had been the stuff of legends. There were rumors running rampant at Crave—and beyond—about his prowess. About how he rarely went with the same man twice, refused dates, offers to be taken on vacation.

Paulo heard the rumors before he'd ever laid eyes on the man and those alone had made him want to meet Law.

The one making the rounds at the time was that a wealthy businessman from New York flew down on weekends just for time in Law's bed. That he'd offered Law trips in private jets to the Caribbean, had offered him everything, but Law refused. That the businessman hadn't been the first to make him those kinds of offers.

Paulo knew now that it wasn't true—at least it didn't happen more than once. But when Paulo saw Law for the first time, he understood immediately. He just gave off the air of a bad boy—it wasn't faked. It was an I-don't-give-a-fuck attitude mixed with blond hair, blue eyes, rugged good looks. Tall, lean-muscled…he screamed sex. Always looked like he'd just been fucking, too—his hair tousled, a glint in his eye, the smile that was slow to come…but once it did, holy hell, that was all it took for Paulo.

And he'd never been easy to please. Not like this.

Paulo remembered muttering something after Law blew him about a fucking fantasy come true.

Law had looked up at him. "Is that what I am to you—a fantasy? Because if I'm that to you, you're more fucked up than I thought."

Paulo had just smiled and yanked Law on top of him. It was hot and rough and it had been everything Paulo had been hoping for.

The man lived up to the hype, probably because he hadn't been hyping himself. Law never talked about his exploits to anyone, as Paulo soon learned.

He'd found out soon enough that Law appreciated him not spreading the word either. In fact, Law had told him it was one of the reasons he'd seen Paulo again.

When Law's eyes had locked on him, Paulo felt it as hard as a physical touch. But the first time Paulo had actually spoken to Law was inside the hospital, away from the vibe of the club.

Law had this way of focusing on you totally—made you feel like you were the most important person in the world both in and out of bed…and so damned safe, when his big body covered Paulo.

Took a lot to make a cop feel safe, but Law managed to.

Paulo had seen him do it in non-sexual situations. The first time was when he saw Law refuse to leave Kevin's side at the hospital. Kevin had been attacked and raped outside of Crave by JP, a man Law ultimately helped to take down. Paulo had listened in and heard Law telling Kevin that it wasn't his fault, that he should go get some counseling and never let it fuck with his head.

Paulo had assumed Law had firsthand knowledge on the subject. And he had, in a way, lived through Damon's gang rape and borne the guilt.

Now, Paulo was able to put together more details—that fact that Styx disappeared the night Damon had been hurt and how all that tragedy was rolled together for Law.

But that first day into night they'd spent together after Paulo propositioned him at the diner, neither had talked about their childhoods—it was something Paulo almost studiously avoided bringing up.

Instead, Law talked about the club, what often happened behind the scenes… He'd been so damned entertaining.

And they'd talked movies—Law loved them—new and old. Music, too, and he'd approved of Paulo's collection.

They'd fucked to Foghat and then some Barry White that made Law laugh.

In between, Law talked to him a bit about the military, what it had been like qualifying for Delta, but he'd avoided talk of combat. Paulo understood—once you'd been in it, you didn't want to discuss any of it.

The man had scars on his body and that first morning, he'd moved a little stiffly when he'd woken up. Paulo wanted to question him, especially when he'd noticed the old cigarette burns on Law's hip, but he hadn't.

One of Paulo's first busts as a detective had included a horrific case of child abuse—he'd learned more on the subject than he'd ever wanted to know.

He'd given Law a couple of Advil and water—Law had narrowed his eyes at that but he'd taken it—and then Paulo had pulled Law back into bed and given him a massage that turned to sex.

And then he'd done some investigating, but that had happened later, after Law had been hurt. Paulo had stumbled on some information that led him to more—and although he was pissed at himself that he'd done it, it had given him an immediate understanding of many things concerning Law.

Now, Styx was telling him there was more to the story. More than living with broken bones and broken dreams through most of childhood, and Jesus, he had to stop thinking about those details in the file because they made him sick and angry all at once.

He checked out the side window, saw Paulo and Law pacing and talking…obviously, they were still fighting.

Restlessly, he prowled the house, stopping when he hit the front door. He looked beyond the curtain toward the woods. It was dark and it was snowing and maybe he'd just seen a shadow of nothing…

But no…something—someone—was out there. Fuck.

He grabbed a pair of binoculars Styx had left on the kitchen table and used them as surreptitiously as possible. Honed in on a man lying on the ground, covered in snow, with a rifle and a scope, pointing in Law and Styx's direction.

The shooter was so busy trying to get a clean shot at both men together that he didn't see Paulo taking aim with the hunting rifle he took from the table in favor of his pistol, which he shoved into the back of his jeans. He was intimately aquatinted with rifles from his youth, could take down a buck at one hundred yards. Perps, too.

He took advantage of the window in the bathroom that gave him a good shot. He eased it open carefully, could hear Law and Styx talking loudly. He placed the rifle on the ledge and his hands steadied—he was grateful that Law and Styx were arguing physically, because had they been standing still, the shooter wouldn't be hesitating.

There wasn't time to be nervous any longer. Paulo aimed right between the eyes, and the shot rang through the air and hit its mark. He remained in place, waiting to see if the man moved again, even as Styx and Law came running through the back door.

They were in and safe. Paulo left the rifle, and he pulled his pistol out of his pocket and ran out the front door, aware that Styx was following behind him. Paulo headed to the man he'd shot, his cop's instinct kicking in hard, went to his knees and felt for a pulse.

None. He rolled the man, saw the mark between his eyes—a damned good and clean shot—and was checking for ID when Styx knelt next to him.

"Check the woods, Law." Styx handed Law his gun and in that moment, Paulo looked up and saw the jungle in Law's eyes, the soldier readying for recon.

"Hey, Paulo, you okay?" Styx was asking, and Paulo turned from watching Law's back into the dark green eyes of the man in front of him.

"Fine. You recognize him?"

"No."

Paulo handed him the perp's wallet and Styx looked through it. "I'll call Tomcat to run it, but this means we're made. We've got to try to outrun this storm."

"And hope this guy's working alone," Paulo said grimly.

Paulo hadn't hesitated—the shot was clean, decisions made in what was no doubt mere seconds, and Styx had seen agency guys crack under similar pressure.

Instead, Paulo had thrived and had continued to keep control of the situation…until he'd realized how close the man lying dead on the ground had come to killing Law and started to lose it a little. Styx could see it in his face when he'd looked up into Law's.

But once Styx gave him a job, he'd snapped to. "Paulo, head inside and start packing whatever you can into the truck. We're out of here ASAP."

Paulo nodded, took his pistol and moved fast across the lawn as Law came out of the woods.

"Woods are clear. Found his truck parked up the road and partially into the woods." Law held some papers. "Registration and insurance under the name Donald Orlandi."

Styx didn't have to ask if Law had wiped his prints.

"Looks like he came alone. Doesn't mean he didn't broadcast this intel to everyone," Law continued. "Is your father known to work with a group?"

"He definitely outsources," Styx confirmed. "We've got to bolt. I'll take care of the body—help Paulo pack the truck. Take everything. Once we find a new place, we're not leaving for a while."

"You got this?" Law looked between the body and Styx, and when he nodded, Law took off toward the house.

Styx covered the body hurriedly and decided to leave the guy's truck where he'd parked it, well out of sight. There wasn't enough time to do what he wanted to do right now, but he could work with this.

Paulo and Law had worked fast. They'd stripped the house, taking everything they could, including the gasoline so they wouldn't have to stop as often. The three men got into the truck, Styx insisting they remain in the back, even though the windows were heavily darkened.

The storm had started to take hold—blizzard-like conditions popped up very quickly, and Styx moved along in the heavy truck, needing to put as much space between him and the old safe house as possible.

"There has to be a leak, Styx," Paulo said finally, and Styx nodded, the possibility of who and why having rolled around in his mind since he'd buried the man under snow and leaves.

"It's not Tomcat," he said finally, and Paulo agreed. Law was strangely silent and the tension radiating off him was understandable.

Styx finally called Tomcat.

"Problem?"

"Big time." He filled the man in quickly, heard him cursing on the other end of the line. "We're headed farther up."

"Good. You let me know when you stop. You check in with me every half an hour." Tomcat sounded angry and he never hid that emotion when someone wronged Styx, something Styx always appreciated.

"I have a name on the registration." He read the information as he kept an eye on the road.

"I'll dispatch a cleaner to take care of everything," Tomcat promised. "You're all okay?"

"Yeah."

"Tell Paulo he did good. And check in," Tomcat said, and Styx hung the phone up and put it in the cup holder. It was time for both hands on the wheel.

They were quiet as hell for the next part of the drive, with Styx and Law and Paulo all watching their sixes, but after a while it became apparent they hadn't been followed.

And three exhausting hours later, he pulled onto a small road that had no signs to alert anyone there was even a road, let alone a house in these parts.

The safe house was one Styx and Tomcat had used in the

early days. Styx kept up on the bills so he knew the heat was on and the water was running. He'd hired a groundskeeper to look after the place and it had been mortgaged under a fake name.

He barely got the car up the driveway but managed to get it into the attached garage he and Tomcat had built for this specific purpose. It was steel-lined, and he breathed a sigh of relief as the door closed down behind them and the light in the garage flickered on.

"No generator, but we've got flashlights and a fireplace if we lose power." The way the light was going in and out with the wind, that would happen soon.

"I'll start the fire." Paulo started grabbing the wood stored along the wall in the garage under a tarp. He heaved some logs and went inside after Styx unlocked the doors.

Styx checked in with Tomcat and then set a few battery-powered alarms around the place.

There was no way out now and, from the looks of things, no way in.

Styx and Law carried in the rest of the stuff in silence, and by the time the food was in the fridge and the other supplies laid out, Paulo had a nice fire going.

It was just in time, too, because the lights sputtered and died. Styx grabbed a few lanterns from the closet, put them in the kitchen and the living room.

"This couch pulls out," he said. "I've got a sleeping bag for the floor."

"I'm going to shower before we lose the hot water." Paulo took one of the lanterns and found his way to a bathroom. He hadn't stopped to grab any clothing but there were plenty of towels.

Paulo had saved them both, but he was still freaked—and pissed, no doubt, at the way Law continued to ignore him.

"He's pissed."

"So am I." Law was pulling out the sofa bed, putting on sheets. "He should never have dug around my past like that."

"He loves you," Styx said, like that explained everything, and it probably did, but Law never wanted anyone to know his vulnerabilities. "Would you have ever told him?"

"I don't know…it was all so new."

"Not really—for you, it's a relationship, whether you want to admit it or not. But I guess the less you admit, the less you'll have to take responsibility for your fuck-ups."

Law sighed. "I'm too fucking tired to fight anymore."

"Too tired to thank Paulo for saving your life?"

Law didn't answer that and just got into the bed he'd made, turning his back on Styx. Styx, in turn, put a throwaway phone next to him. "At least call Damon and check in—he won't be suspicious if you're a prick."

He walked into the kitchen, ignoring Law's muttered curses as he went.

Law was still muttering every curse he knew at Styx—mainly pissed at himself the entire time—while he dialed Damon.

Damon picked up after a few rings, sounding more relaxed than Law had ever heard him. For Tanner to get the leave had been tough, but Damon had called in some favors and yes, the men needed that time away together.

Tanner would go back out with Delta and be gone on secret missions that both Damon and Law knew far too much about—which was really the main problem for Damon, who'd already lost a lover to military action—but they'd finally come to an understanding.

Tanner would do his job and Damon would stay behind and be a miserable son of a bitch to everyone in his path—including and especially Law—until Tanner returned.

To see Damon happy, Law was more than okay with that trade.

"We've been eating and drinking and sightseeing," Damon was telling him.

"I'm sure that's not all," Law said, and Damon snorted and Tanner said hi in the background. And he thought things were going to go smoothly until Damon demanded, "What's wrong?" and fuck it all, the man was better than a lie detector.

Law would have to make this work by telling some half-truths and pretending something other than what was wrong was actually wrong. Because if he couldn't throw Damon off the scent completely, he'd just confuse the shit out of him instead. "Nothing."

"It's Paulo, isn't it?"

Well goddamn, that was a big part of it. He sighed in spite of himself and Damon muttered something under his breath.

"It's Paulo."

"I know you went to see him the night Tanner and I left."

"Yeah, I did."

"Still pushing him away?"

"I don't know what to do, Damon," he said honestly. "If I'm not pushing him, he's pushing me."

"Sounds familiar."

"You and Tanner got past it way more quickly than me and Paulo—we haven't gotten past anything." He tried not to think about how pissed he'd been—how he'd walked out on both him and Styx.

How he still hadn't said he was sorry to either man.

"Go to him. What's stopping you?" Damon paused. "You can't still be thinking about him."

He looked toward the kitchen, heard Styx moving around in there and knew the man was listening to the entire conversation. "If Styx came back—"

Damon snorted at the thought. "Okay, I'll play—if Styx came back, would you give Paulo up?"

Styx walked back into the living room as Law said, "No—I couldn't give Paulo up for him. I couldn't give Styx up for Paulo, either."

"Like Styx would go for that."

Law and Styx hadn't discussed it at all last night, but the fact that Styx had walked into the room and watched… well, Law had no doubt he remembered. "We used to do threesomes all the time."

"One-offs," Damon said, as if he needed reminding.

Law knew that his deepest, darkest secrets, needs, fantasies—they were all safe with Damon. They would be so with Styx as well, and he had to believe that Paulo could handle them.

And this was a sudden, deep, dark craving, something he never thought possible. Those times in his past were one-offs, yes, Damon was correct. But what he wanted now he knew wouldn't happen only once…not if he allowed it to happen at all.

But something inside him knew he couldn't stop it any more than he could stop a speeding train.

"I couldn't say no to either of them," Law said quietly, aware that Styx was watching him, the expression on his face hard to read, shadowed by the flickering firelight. "I wouldn't want them to say no to each other. Do you think that's too much to ask?"

He was speaking to Damon but staring at Styx as he spoke the words. Styx wasn't saying anything and, on his end, Damon went silent for a long second. "I've never seen a threesome work for very long, Law. But if anyone could handle it…"

"Do you really think it could work?" He heard the urgency in his own voice, didn't want to make Damon suspicious. "Forget it—just a fantasy, I guess."

"I think you could, Law, if it made all of you happy." Damon paused. "Do you need me to come home?"

"For what? To watch me mope? You and Tanner have a blast—check in, okay?"

"Okay…we'll talk soon." Damon hung up the phone and Law cursed inwardly for many different reasons.

Law hated lying to Damon. But he wasn't about to ruin the man's vacation. If this wasn't figured out by the time Damon returned, then all hell would break loose.

He handed the phone back to Styx, who slid it into his pocket and then walked past Law and into the bathroom where Paulo was still showering.

Talk about all hell breaking loose…

Whether Law did it purposely or not, he was testing Styx—and this was one test he would pass with flying fucking colors.

If Law wanted him—needed him—to invite Paulo in, Styx would do so. It wouldn't be a hardship and he'd been attracted to the younger man from the first.

He didn't bother to knock when he entered the bedroom and then went toward the bathroom adjacent to it. That door was open and he glanced inside, forgetting there were clear glass doors on the showers here. With the lantern on the sink, Styx could see Paulo clearly, sucked in a breath when he saw the tats displayed beautifully along the man's lean, muscled back and arms, the colors and designs rippling with the taut muscles underneath them.

As he watched, Paulo squeezed the washcloth so the soap ran in rivulets down his back, over the very tightly muscled ass, down his thighs and calves. Stood for a few minutes with his head down, palms on the tiles so the water could cascade down his neck.

Paulo was hard, too, despite all that had happened tonight. Styx had been hard from the second he'd walked into the room. And then suddenly, Paulo stood and turned his head toward Styx, the look on his face letting Styx know he'd been busted for a while.

Styx didn't care, didn't move, watched Paulo shut off the water and walk out of the shower. He toweled off but he didn't wrap the towel around his waist, flung it to the floor instead and crossed the floor until he stood toe to toe with Styx.

"I can handle this," was all he said.

With his hair slicked back, his eyes glowed and Styx fought to keep his composure. "You don't have to pretend you're okay. You're freaked. Why?"

"I almost lost you both."

"I'm not your responsibility." Styx regretted the words as soon as they came out of his mouth, mainly because they weren't true…but the look in Paulo's face reminded him of the way he'd felt when Law accused him of lying.

"That's right—you're not." Paulo went to brush past him but Styx grabbed him, braced for Paulo to start swinging, but he didn't.

This wasn't a lost boy, not completely. No, he was a grown man and a hell of a lot more honest about his feelings than either Styx or Law. "Do you want me to be?"

Paulo stared at him, handsome, proud. "I thought I did, but not when you're being a prick."

"My SOP," Styx said quietly as the air changed between them, nearly crackled as the image of Paulo, bound and spread, flashed before his eyes. "Can you handle it?"

"You and Law both think you're so hard to handle." Paulo laughed a little. "You're both way more transparent than you think."

"To the right person. And you're one of them?"

"If you want to find out, keep pushing."

A challenge. Styx had walked in on him in the shower purposefully, and what had he expected from that? For Paulo to cry modesty, wrap up in a towel and run?

Paulo stood, wet, naked, totally unapologetic and ready, his stance a taunt.

He was calling Styx's bluff, raised his chin as Styx took the time to appraise him. Both men were hard—Styx couldn't deny it any more than Paulo could, because he was obviously straining the front of his worn jeans, the bulge unmistakable.

Styx reached out and traced the tats on one of Paulo's arms with a finger. They were a mix of intricate swirls and tribal designs, some black and grayscale with touches of color…it was all fucking beautiful. He had full sleeves to the elbows and his back piece was on its way to being complete, but his chest was clear. "You saved Law—you saved me. I couldn't be more grateful, you know."

"I believe that. What about the asshole in the other room?" Paulo shot back.

"Not ready to stop being an asshole yet." Styx realized the younger man had started to shiver. "You ever killed someone in the line of duty?"

"Yeah."

"Did you freak out the first time?"

"I fucked up the first time and got my partner shot. I never made that mistake again," Paulo bit out. "This is too much—you can't focus on keeping Law safe with this shit. The two of you need to spend time together, dealing with each other. I'll go to another safe house."

Styx believed he would do that, would make the sacrifice for Law, and it was the last thing any of them wanted. It just took Law's call to Damon to put it into perspective.

"You can't go off on your own, Paulo. Besides, you're not the problem."

"I'm not a prisoner, am I?"

Styx gave a small smile as he thought about the way Paulo had been bound to the bed last night. "Not yet. But I can make that happen if you want to be tied down and helpless again."

8

Paulo shivered again, and this time it had nothing to do with the chill from having no heat in the house. The thought of Styx—of Law—tying him down, keeping him…

Fuck. He looked down because he didn't know what the hell to do, or where Styx was going with all of this.

"You saved his life," Styx repeated quietly, cupped Paulo's chin in his palm and forced him to meet his gaze. "You saved mine."

Paulo felt his cheeks flush. Hell, his whole body was on fire. "He loves you. I couldn't let anything happen to you."

"You would give him up if that would make him happy?"

"Yeah, I would."

"That's why he loves you."

"If I hadn't told him that I researched his childhood, he wouldn't have been outside in the line of fire."

"Bullshit." Styx's words were firm, but his eyes were kind. The man with no childhood and teenage memories before the age of sixteen had been clinging to the memories of Law all these years, and Paulo could understand that.

"I haven't known him long…but I understand why you love him," Paulo said.

"I understand why he loves you."

"He doesn't, Styx. I've been competing with you from the start."

"It's not about competition," Styx said. "The heart doesn't compete in bullshit—it just tells it like it is and we have to be ready to listen."

Styx's arms circled him, tugged him close and it was all over. He couldn't resist this man any more than he could Law.

Law, who was on the other side of the door, pissed as hell at him.

He focused his attention back on the man in front of him, had wondered if there would be this kind of attraction between him and Styx without Law.

The answer, of course, was yes. Holy motherfucker, yes. Styx's body was hot—it was like being close to an inferno, but he didn't mind getting burned.

Styx didn't kiss him—but he wanted the man to do so… and his blood rushed hot to his groin at the first contact of their bodies.

This had been coming—the close proximity, the fighting—Paulo knew it would lead to this. But as much as he wanted Styx…he didn't want to lose Law. And so he went to pull back but Styx cupped a hand around the back of his neck…another slid down the front of his jeans, and

Paulo knew resistance was futile.

Law had described Styx as his drug and Paulo knew why…Styx was larger than life. When he was in the room, he ate up all the oxygen, made you feel like you were swimming through a thick haze.

He was handsome, yes, but it was more than that.

Styx was insistent and Paulo didn't want to say no. He'd seen the way Styx manhandled Law and he wanted that. And, as if in response, Styx pulled back a little, his hand circling Paulo's cock, and Paulo bucked into his palm.

"Good boy," Styx crooned, and Paulo didn't care what the man called him as long as he could come and release some of this tension. "Just remember, you call me old man again, and I will put you over my knee."

Jesus. Paulo's knees nearly buckled at the mention of that, the way they had last night and why was the thought of that actually happening making him weak?

Styx smiled, like he knew and wasn't telling.

Paulo wanted to concede to everything, but he couldn't. "I'm not doing anything with you…because of Law."

"What if it's something Law wants?"

At the sound of Law's voice asking the question, Paulo started, looked between the two men. "How the hell is that supposed to work?"

"I don't know," Law admitted. "But I refuse to lose either of you."

Law had watched the two men almost from the moment Paulo walked out of the shower. Styx was tender to Paulo. Paulo looked wrecked.

And Law knew he'd most definitely been an asshole, had barely looked at Paulo during the drive. Knew he needed to apologize, to own his shit, but he hadn't been able to let it go.

Until now. Because what was happening in front of him made his mouth go dry and his dick hard.

Styx brought his mouth down on Paulo's, and Law watched the seduction begin. It fucking took his breath away watching the men kiss, with Styx's hand on the back of Paulo's head, another on his bare ass, and the mix of Styx fully clothed and Paulo naked and all the tattoos was incredible.

Paulo resisted—at first. But it wasn't easy to do with Styx—not at all—and then Paulo's hands went to Styx's face and held it. Paulo was responding, because he needed to, wanted to, and Law understood why. Finally, Paulo moved his hands to Styx's shoulders, twined them in his hair as the kisses became harder, more intense. Styx's hands were on Paulo's ass, pushing him closer, and Law wondered what Styx would do to the younger man first. Couldn't wait to see, actually.

But he wanted to be a part of it more. So he walked into the room and Paulo broke the kiss and stared at him.

"Fuck, Law, I'm…"

"It's all right." Law moved forward, stood next to the men who'd started to break apart and stopped that. "Don't stop. Please."

Paulo looked half stunned, confused as Law guided Styx's head back towards his. Styx wasn't half as confused, began kissing Paulo again until the man gave up worrying and went with it. Maybe it was because Law kept his hand on Paulo's shoulder. Whispered in his ear, "You look so fucking hot."

He heard Paulo moan against Styx's mouth and his cock jumped, because this was the way it needed to be right now. He had atoning to do, and somehow this felt right. He needed Styx, but he couldn't be with him alone.

He needed Paulo, needed to find a way to forgive him for prying, for discovering things about Law that he'd never wanted anyone else to know, and this was the way. It had never felt this right before.

Paulo tried to pull back a little, but Styx took Paulo in hand again, this time more powerfully so Paulo squirmed then settled into the kiss, especially as Law moved behind him and kissed along the back of his neck. Whispered, "That's it, baby—give yourself to Styx…to me."

And then he sank to his knees and pushed Paulo's thighs apart. Licked a path up Paulo's thigh and spread Paulo's ass, began to tongue along his crack, and Paulo trembled like he couldn't hold himself up.

Styx took the same position as Law in front of Paulo, and Law knew he'd take Paulo's cock in his mouth, knew the second he did it because both men held fast to Paulo so he wouldn't drop.

Law redoubled his efforts, spearing his tongue and entering Paulo, heard his cries above him. It was *Law* and *Styx* and *holy fuck* and God, Law wanted to fuck him immediately.

But this was about Paulo now and no one else. And when Paulo came in Styx's mouth, he let out a yell that seemed to reverberate through the entire cabin, let the orgasm rock his entire body for what seemed an eternity.

When he'd quieted and all Law heard was his riotous breathing, Law carried Paulo out to the bed in front of the fire and the two of them lay on the mattress with Paulo between them.

Styx was at Paulo's back this time and Law nodded over the man's shoulder, communicating that this needed to continue…that he wasn't ready to be with Styx alone yet.

It was all centering on him, and for sure, Paulo didn't mind being part of their avoidance technique. Unless you were a goddamned idiot, no red-blooded American gay man was going to miss this opportunity.

If he closed his eyes, he could tell Styx's touch from Law's. Styx's was rougher, although both men were especially good in the manhandling department, as evidenced by the way they tied him down by his wrists and ankles so he was on his back, spread and open to them, unable to stop them from doing whatever they wanted to him.

"He likes it rough," Law murmured, and Styx smiled and Paulo said nothing because he was still partially incoherent from the rimming/blowjob experience.

"Going to relieve some more of that stress," Styx told him. Paulo tried to argue that he had none but he gave up when Styx sucked a nipple hard between his tongue and teeth, and Law played with the other between his fingers.

He heard the ripping of condom packages and knew what would happen next. Could barely stand to wait for it, either.

And then Styx went down on him, took Paulo's balls in his mouth and suckled them, used his fingers to apply pressure to his perineum, and that drove him out of his goddamned mind with need and want. Styx knew it, played there while his hand circled Paulo's cock, which was impossibly hard again, despite the recent orgasm.

And then Styx rose up and entered him without warning, taking a long, slow slide, his piercing adding that extra brush to his gland that nearly drove him into the ceiling as Law watched.

"Yeah, he's good at that—taking your ass and making it his," Law told him. "You don't have a choice in the matter. He can do anything he goddamned pleases—and he will."

"Law." The name, moaned out because looking and listening to Law while Styx had his way made Paulo's need to come again immediate.

"Go ahead—no one's stopping you," Law murmured. "But no one's untying you yet. We need more than two orgasms to bring you back to an even keel."

Paulo came hard—Styx continued to pump and grind even as the contractions rocked Paulo's body.

Law was watching Styx now, his face tight with a lust of his own, and when Styx came with a near howl and stilled, Law pushed him off and entered Paulo. The mattress shook as Law gripped Paulo's hips, and Paulo finally understood the truth behind the term *fucking you blind*, because it was going to happen. His senses went into overload and when he shot between them, Styx moved in to lick the come from his belly and Law plunged into him harder, and there was nothing Paulo could do to make it stop.

And the best part was, he had no desire to do so.

In the aftermath, the scene was very much like it had been the night before when he'd panicked. But this time, he was simply boneless, drained, and he didn't mind the men fussing over him. Both had washcloths and they toweled him dry before crawling into bed on either side of him.

"Thinking of untying me anytime soon?" Paulo asked

finally, when he could actually form words.

"Yeah—and then retying you in a different position," Styx said, and the man was one hundred percent serious. Paulo supposed that's what he got for asking.

9

Law did untie Paulo then, rubbed his arms to bring the circulation back into them. Styx did the same thing with Paulo's legs, and Law did have plans to strap Paulo back to the bed and take him again. And again.

But first, there was still some making up he needed to do. He lay back against the pillow and Paulo turned to him, burying his face against Law's shoulder. Styx watched the two of them, jerked his head toward the bedroom, asking silently if Law wanted him to leave.

Fuck, he didn't. He shook his head, and Paulo lifted his and looked between the men. Law sat up against the back of the couch that served as a headboard for the pull-out bed, wanting all the heaviness to just leave his heart.

There was so much he needed to put behind him, to forgive, that if he didn't start he would break from bitterness.

How often did anyone get second chances like this?

"I know what you read in my file," he started. "But I need to tell you about it."

Paulo just nodded, and Law knew the younger man

would never make him, but Styx probably would. And Styx would've been right. Talking it through to both men seemed so right. And despite all the other shit falling down around their heads, tonight there was nothing more to do but put some ghosts to rest.

"I had an older brother," he started, glanced at Paulo, who'd sat up facing him. Styx moved in closer, like their proximity would keep him from breaking down—and maybe it would. "He wasn't much older than me and we weren't really close, but if I didn't have him growing up, I probably wouldn't have survived the abuse. Because it was hell. There were days I just wanted to die. Prayed for it, and probably would've done it, but I wouldn't leave my brother like that."

Even though he and his brother had been mostly adversarial, when it came to the beatings, they never sold one another out. A completely dysfunctional relationship, and Law was sure it couldn't have been any different, considering the circumstances. "I knew early on that my preference was for men and my brother couldn't understand that. I guess he thought it might make him gay by association, but I was grateful he let me tell him."

"The file says you guys were moved to foster care," Paulo said quietly. "How did the system fail you so badly?"

Had it? Looking back, Law supposed it did, but back then, what he'd always known was the only thing he'd been comfortable with, even though he knew it wasn't normal.

"We were taken away twice, but those places were as bad as home. It's why I started working at Greg's to begin with. I needed money if I was going to get out and escape foster care, and Greg hired me even though I was young. Paid me cash. My brother didn't want to work with fags, as he so eloquently referred to me, but he put in his time bussing at a diner. Our grades sucked because we barely made it in, but it wasn't like anyone at home cared. After a while, our parents didn't notice that we'd unplugged the phone from the wall. They were too busy drinking and taking their anger out on us."

Law rubbed his hip, remembering the day his father burned him with the cigarettes while Law stood there, too goddamned stubborn to cry out and give his father that satisfaction. "In the end, it was daily. Greg knew. It was impossible to hide. The broken collarbone…Greg was the one who took me to the ER. Paid cash for the visit. For a while, my father tried to hit us where no one would see, but he stopped caring. We just hung around a few days too long. We had bus tickets out of the city. We had cash. We were packed."

Law could still see his brother's suitcase if he thought about it hard enough—it was sitting next to the window, ready for them to head out the window and down the fire escape.

He wasn't sure if he could get the next words out, but it was the missing piece of the puzzle Paulo didn't know.

"The file listed your brother as a runaway. What happened to him?" Paulo asked, and that gave Law the push he needed.

"My father killed him. I don't think he meant to go that far—not at that moment—but he pushed Jason down the stairs and by the time he hit the bottom, he was dead."

He could close his eyes and still see the odd angle of his brother's head, the opened eyes that held a surprised, scared look. The screams of his mother…not because she'd lost her son, but because she feared she'd go to jail. "I left that night. I don't know where he's buried. The police never found him—the school reported us both missing and as far as I know, they assumed we were just runaways. I would've turned him in—maybe I should have. When I was old enough to think about telling the police everything, I discovered that both my parents were dead, and there was never any justice anyway."

And there it was, his famous past, laid out for both men to see. He was sure the pain of it was etched on his face and his body felt tight from holding everything together.

When Paulo spoke, there wasn't a trace of pity. "I wanted to find out why you were always in pain in the morning… or when it was damp out." He touched Law's hip, and Law jerked away, ashamed of the burns that were still there.

"I knew I didn't want to get close to you," he muttered.

"Because I'd see everything. Expose you." Paulo pulled him back and Law finally met his eyes. "I love what I see.

I just hate that you had to suffer through what you did to make it here. I wish I could wave a wand and erase it or at least get rid of the memories, but I can't. I hate that you went through it. But you wouldn't be who I love if that hadn't happened. Should I wish that away?"

"No," Law said, the word spilling out without thought. It was all about feelings now, and it had never quite been like this for him, and the word love came so naturally, so unabashedly from Paulo that it moved him more than he'd thought possible. He let both men move closer to him. With their bodies on either side of him, he felt warm and safe. "I made it out."

"You paid a hell of a price," Styx told him.

"I've had more good years than bad," Law said.

"Fuck, Law, no one should have had any years like that." Paulo rubbed the back of Law's neck. "You didn't deserve that shit."

Styx buried his head against Law's shoulder and Law bowed his head. "What do either of you see in me?"

Styx's head shot up and he took Law by the chin. "I see everything, Law. Goddamn it, you are fucking everything to me."

He leaned in and kissed Law on the forehead and then touched his forehead to Law's. Paulo kept his hand on the back of the man's neck, whispered. "You're the best."

After a long moment, Law turned his attention back to Paulo. "I'm sorry I was a prick."

"Fuck, I—"

"Don't want to talk more about it now. Right now, I want to fuck you while Styx fucks me. I need that."

"I need that too," Paulo whispered, and that was all Law wanted to hear. He bent to kiss Paulo's shoulder and then the man's lips softly.

"You're going to be sore as hell," Law told him.

"Don't care—worth it," Paulo urged him, and then Paulo gasped in surprise and bucked against Law. Styx had a small smile on his face and his hand was on Paulo's ass, fingering him, preparing him for Law.

He knew Styx was being gentle, could tell by the look of pleasure and not pain on Paulo's face. And Law knew he would have to move closer to Styx, to surrender to him this time, and it scared the shit out of him. Paulo seemed to understand, was caressing Law's shoulders, sucking his nipples, waiting patiently for Law to make the first move even as he undulated from Styx's machinations.

Law finally tried to push Paulo to his stomach, but the younger man shook his head as Styx shifted to let things begin.

"Want to watch," Paulo said, and Law nodded and started kissing him, forgetting everything else but the pleasure he felt.

But it wasn't easy. He tensed when Styx touched him and then Styx moved to leave the two of them. But Paulo stopped him by grabbing his wrist and tugging him back.

"This needs to happen," Paulo told Law, and Law nodded. "Good. Let us make this up to you."

He opened his mouth to tell them it wasn't necessary… but fuck it, on some level, it was. And while Paulo kept him steady, Styx came up behind him and kissed him along his shoulders. Held him in place. Ordered him to, "fuck Paulo now", and that seemed the best idea possible.

Styx had already lubed Paulo, but now he reached around and slicked Law's cock. At the touch, Law let his head fall back against Styx, and Styx murmured something to him that he couldn't quite make out, but it made him smile anyway. Maybe it was *baby* or *love you* or a combination of both, said in that special growl that warmed him.

And then Styx pushed him forward gently and Law spread Paulo's legs and entered him. Paulo arched his back at the intrusion, clutched the sheets but kept his eyes on Law.

Law went slowly, not wanting to hurt the man who'd already had his share of filling that night—and the night before. But Paulo was insistent, telling him, "More, Law… come on…take me," and Law did, pushed inside until he was buried completely and Paulo clung to him as he began to move against him. Styx was still there behind him, waiting and watching, rubbing Law's back.

And then Styx started to touch him and everything changed. The electricity pulsed through him—and the fear and he didn't want to want Styx that much…didn't want to want Paulo, either.

But these men weren't letting him off the hook, seemed to sense his need to run, and instead of letting him, they pressed him between them and urged him forward.

Slowly, he accepted.

Paulo stared between the men. Both had been through hell.

Both beautiful. Handsome. Strong.

Survivors.

Paulo wanted both of them again with an ache that was indescribable. Wanted to help both men feel better...or at least, simply feel.

He stroked Law's abs and knew Law would surrender by the sudden spike of heat in the room.

Law had bonded Paulo and Styx together—now it was time for them to heal the rift they couldn't afford to let grow any wider. Here, they were safe. Now was all they had, and they would need to take full advantage of it.

Paulo willed himself not to think of the future, but only of right this moment.

Law was still deep inside him—and rock hard. As Paulo watched, Styx sucked along Law's shoulder, leaving a red mark that he laved over with a lick to soothe. He looked up and smiled at Paulo and then Law's eyes closed, his body tensed…and then his head dropped back and he murmured, *fuck yeah*, and rocked his hips.

Styx was fingering him and Paulo was only too happy to enjoy the show. Law's carved abs combined with Styx's muscled forearm around Law's shoulders.

"Give him more," Paulo urged and Styx must've complied because Law drew in a sharp breath and stilled for a long second.

"Good, baby?" Styx asked and Law managed a small nod of his head. "You're so goddamned tight."

Law groaned in response, and Paulo could only imagine it had been a long time since the man bottomed. It would be interesting to watch Law switch.

For Styx, Paulo imagined that Law didn't switch at all. Then again, Law could be damned persuasive when he wanted to be, and that could be a whole other fantasy Paulo tucked away.

"You ready for me?" Styx asked quietly, and Law turned to look at him. Styx captured his mouth with a kiss and God, they were fucking beautiful together. And when they broke apart, Law leaned forward, held Paulo's legs apart and thrust, cock brushing his prostate, until Paulo's eyes rolled to the back of his head, and then Styx entered Law and the whole rhythm changed. Law wasn't in control anymore—and of all of them, he was a slave to the sensations, unable to do more than rut whenever Styx pounded him.

To watch Law give it up like that was fascinating to Paulo.

Law had already mentioned he was a switch, but to see the submission, to watch him give himself over completely, was the hottest thing Paulo had seen to date.

Paulo was given no quarter either—being fucked by both of them as Styx set the pace. Listening to Styx talk dirty dialed up the experience.

"Yeah, that's it, Law…can't do anything but take it… letting me into that tight ass…so tight and all for me."

Law seemed mesmerized by what was happening and Paulo loved seeing it unfold. He reached to hold Law's shoulders as Styx leaned against Law heavily, holding his legs open, his own arousal unmistakable and his orgasm barely contained if the way his neck muscles strained was any indication.

Paulo bucked up to drive Law deeper, and the vibrations echoed through all three men. Styx pushed back and Paulo groaned and grasped at Law's hips. "More," he told them. "Don't fucking stop."

They didn't, Styx setting a rhythm that allowed each man to gain maximum pleasure. Paulo nearly lost his mind every time Law's cock hit his prostate—it was almost too much and he had the least control of any of the men. Had to lie there and take it…could think of nothing better.

Paulo was going to come first—Styx could see it in his eyes. He pumped Law, who was still suffering from a bad case of nerves, which Styx could well understand.

None of this was solely about sex—it never really had been.

Styx hadn't made any promises that he wasn't leaving Law again, not like before. But what that meant for the three of them remained to be seen.

"Come on, babe, you first," Law told Paulo, and the younger man complied willingly, his orgasm seeming to take him by surprise with its strength. Considering how many times the man had already climaxed, Styx was surprised he was even semicoherent.

His stress level was definitely at a manageable level, the earlier horror of the morning—and Law's confessions—momentarily pushed to the background.

Now that Paulo was under control, Styx wasn't ready to let go of Law—not yet. And as Law pulled out of Paulo and Paulo curled up on his side, breathing hard, he remained inside Law's ass with Law kneeling in front of him.

Seeing Law on his hands and knees, head hanging, biceps and forearms stretched taut and his heavy sex and balls hanging between his legs…fuck, it was all he could do not to come immediately.

But he wanted it to last.

"Now it's your turn—only yours," he told Law, heard the man's sharp intake of breath, but there was no further resistance. And while Paulo watched the men, Styx took Law, roughly and Law moaned for him—all pleasure.

He rocked into Law, hard and fast enough to make him cry out and grab onto the edge of the bed to hold himself up.

And then Styx pulled out and flipped to his back, and Law held his breath. Stared into those green eyes that watched him with more tenderness than he'd ever deserved, and then Law put his hands up to Styx's shoulders and pulled him down into a kiss.

God, it was beautiful—not a kiss with fight in it, but one of total surrender. And when Law spoke, his words were harsh, but his tone wasn't. "Are we really…going to do this? Are you staying, Styx? Or are you going to rip my fucking heart out again?"

It was a fair question and it made Styx wince. "I want to. But if you're asking me not to deal with my father…don't ask. Because I have to, if nothing else, for all the years I wasted not being with you. And the thought of you being with other men…"

"Like you haven't been?" Law shot back.

"You've bottomed for them."

"Trying to remember what you felt like," Law told him. "Every fucking night I jerk myself off and try to remember what you felt like."

Styx stilled, brought his hands up to cup Law's face. "Every night I wanted you. I never stopped, Law. You have to believe that it ate me up inside. I never forgot about you once."

The man knew the right things to say, and Styx wasn't big on lip service. Law chose to believe him, to understand.

Styx was kissing him—half tender, half fierce, and the mix was enough to make Law want to come then and there. The danger that threatened to do them all in was responsible for this, the heightened adrenaline—the need that made their blood boil.

As teens, lovemaking had been fast and hard and all about satiating pulsing hormones. Now, it was more about an urgency that only came from experience, from knowing that this time could be the last.

Both men had been living on the edge for years, Law in Delta Force and Styx in the CIA, and they both understood and believed in living for the moment.

But Law had never forgotten Styx, never stopped hoping he'd come back into his life in some capacity or another. And he had, so Law was going to hold on and not let go.

"Fuck me, Styx. Take me any way you goddamned want me. Please."

Law had wanted to say those words to Styx's face for what seemed like forever. Seeing the heat flare in Styx's eyes, he decided that it had been worth the wait. The man entered him again without waiting. Law wrapped his legs around Styx and let Styx take him, accepted it all, and there was forgiveness there.

"Sorry, baby," he murmured against Law's mouth. "So fucking sorry…"

"Me too," Law said, and then they were moving so fast together, Styx's head buried in Law's neck as their pace quickened. Grabbed Styx's broad shoulders as the man drove into him, his famous control obviously shot to shit.

They'd both been good, and good together in bed—when they were younger. Time, experience had only improved them both, and the combination proved explosive. The two former club rats were both seasoned warriors, knew all the right places to touch to set each other to implode.

Styx had the same long scar down his back—it hadn't gotten any better with age, and there were a few new ones as well that Law could easily recognize as bullet wounds.

Law had a few himself from his time in combat, knew Styx saw them and that another time, the man would trace them with his tongue and kiss them as if he could make them disappear.

Styx always made him feel as if he'd come home, and tonight was no exception. He buried his face in the man's shoulder and let Styx's hands wander his body.

"Don't stop, Styx. Please…"

And Styx didn't, not for a long time, until Law had come twice, any hesitation long gone.

In the aftermath, Law lay in Styx's arms, unwilling and unable to move. His face was buried against Styx's shoulder, inhaling the smell of the man he'd missed for so long.

Finally, it was right between them, but at some point, Paulo had moved from the bed. Neither man had seen him go.

"Want me to call Paulo in here?" Styx asked and Law nodded, his hands still tight around Styx as if he'd leave again if Law let go. "I'm not going anywhere."

"Making sure."

He heard Styx call for Paulo, heard the younger man pad in and lie on the bed with them. Styx pulled him in close and the three of them lay there together.

"You all right?" Law asked Paulo when he finally lifted his head.

"Yeah, I'm good. Just wanted to give you your space."

"You weren't in the way at all." The fierceness in Styx's voice surprised them all. "I'm the third wheel here."

"I want both of you, dammit," Law said. "And you want each other. So cut the shit and stop ruining my afterglow."

That broke the tension for a few minutes, and Styx pulled Paulo even closer. For the first time in a long time, Law thought he might actually have an unbroken sleep.

10

The days passed with an unsurprising quickness now that the three men had something else to take their minds off the inherent danger in addition to the movies and books once they got power back. Before that, when the blizzard didn't let up for forty-eight hours, leaving them with nothing but candles and a fire, no one complained.

While the power had come back last night, the roads were still impassable, according to Tomcat, and the news left even Styx slightly relaxed.

Law stretched as the closing credits ran on the movie he'd just watched as Paulo slept next to him and Styx read. He wasn't sure what time it was—sometime after midnight, he supposed, but days and nights were mixing up and blending together because it really didn't matter here. What did was that they were safe, and he would do anything he could to stop Styx from going back to his father, even if it was for no other reason than to kill the man. Styx's partner could do that. Law didn't want his lover anywhere near his past.

"I'm going to shower," Styx told him, and Law watched him head to the bathroom. He looked at Paulo, who'd been watching also.

They'd gone ten hours without some kind of sex or blow or hand job. Like a fucking record for them. But every time his gaze settled on one of them, the need blew out, out of his control, and the self-restraint he'd been so proud of all these years collapsed under the reality of the two men who wanted him as badly as he wanted them.

Paulo stirred next to him—once the blanket dropped away, Law noted that the man wore only a pair of shorts. "Guess I missed the movie."

Law ran a hand through the younger man's hair. "The only reason I got to watch it this time was because you slept."

Paulo grinned a little at that. Got out of bed and walked into the bathroom where Styx was showering, brushed his teeth while watching Styx through the glass door.

Law knew because he stood in the doorway, watching Styx soaping himself up, giving his dick a few tugs, and Law's own cock swelled, tenting the sweats he wore.

"Wish that stall was bigger," Paulo murmured as the men contented themselves with simple voyeurism, Law's hands wrapping around Paulo's waist, head resting on his shoulder. "Has he heard from Tomcat?"

"While you slept. Nothing new." Law wasn't sure if that was good or bad at this point. The thought of Styx having to leave again made his heart ache.

Would he stay once all of this was over? No promises had been asked or made either way. It was as if all three men purposely avoided the subject, and after Law had talked about his past, they'd steered away from any potentially upsetting topics.

But their uncertain futures had woken Law up in the middle of the night, unable to move with Paulo's body half on top of him. Styx had been awake too, staring at the ceiling, and they'd eventually drifted back off without talking, but it still bothered him.

Now, Law's erection probed his Paulo's back. "Why don't you lure him to the bedroom? Styx has handcuffs in his bag."

Law snorted but nodded. He waited for Styx to walk out of the stall, stopped him when he grabbed for a towel, sucked some water off a muscled shoulder and continued a long lick down his arm instead.

"I just got clean," Styx told him.

"We'll all get clean again later." Law tugged him toward the bedroom where Paulo was already waiting with two sets of handcuffs. Styx's cock was already responding, had never really gone down despite jerking off in the shower.

"I guess I'm going to be in this state all the time," he muttered.

"Hope you can handle it," Law told him, and Styx in turn grabbed at him and brought him close for a kiss, ground against him until Law groaned in his mouth. His hands trailed down Law's back to his ass, a finger rubbing between his cheeks.

"The young one's getting himself in trouble," he murmured, and Law looked over his own shoulder to see Paulo pouring tequila shots.

"The lemons aren't going to last for much longer," Paulo pointed out, and Styx looked between him and the window, where the snow was blizzarding by, before he downed three in a row and then kissed Law again.

Tequila, lemon, salt and man—oh yeah. Law pushed a little so he and Styx went down on the bed, and then he urged Styx to sit up against the headboard.

"What the hell are you two planning?" Styx asked but didn't have to wait for his answer, because Law and Paulo each took one of his wrists and cuffed it to the headboard. Styx lounged like the king that he was against the pillows they'd set up, and Law sat back on his heels and surveyed the man.

Age had done nothing but been kind to him. The hint of roughness that had been there in his youth was in-your-face, rugged and it turned Law the hell on.

Paulo too, since the younger man was already between Styx's legs, mouth around Styx's cock, and the big man groaned with a rumble in his chest, deep satisfaction. Law ran his hands over Styx's chest, sucked his nipples until he was practically vibrating underneath them.

When he felt Paulo move away, Styx lifted his head.

"Come on, someone take a ride," Styx urged, his grin easy thanks to the shots. He was always relaxed during sex but this was different.

Paulo got on first, and Law watched Styx's cock disappear up his ass and then watched the men together. Paulo was holding Styx and even though Styx was cuffed he was completely, utterly in control. That's who Styx was, what he liked. Bottoming wasn't in his repertoire—he didn't need to give it up the way Law had. And Law was grateful that Styx could be the constant in all of this, although Law knew that if he needed to take Styx, the man would relent.

It would take some coaxing though, and Law wasn't ready for that yet. There were still other hurdles, and for now he just wanted to wallow in the pleasure and forget all the other shit still out there.

He watched the younger man's ass clamp around Styx's cock, his arms wrapped around Styx's shoulders, and Paulo shuddered through his climax. Law tried his best not to come immediately.

Paulo pulled back and kissed Styx, breathing soft moans into his mouth, and Styx kissed him back. When he eased off, Styx surprised him—but not Law—by unlocking the cuffs and coming at Law.

Styx turned him over, put his mouth to his ass and began to fuck it with his tongue as Law begged for mercy. He'd get none, even when he grabbed for the sheets in a frenzy as the sensations grew nearly too much to bear. And then he was calling out Styx's name and some other choice words, even as Styx held his hips fast and ate his ass.

And then there were two tongues—Styx and Paulo working together, licking and laving and driving their tongues inside, one of them licking and sucking his balls…a hand around his cock, stroking firmly and he was going to come, shoot all over himself and the bed. No way around it.

"Not done with you," Styx murmured against his ear, and he just groaned in response, let Styx enter him and ride him hard. He had a fistful of Law's hair in his hand to jerk his head back, exposing the grimace of pain mixed with pleasure he wore…the sounds coming out of his mouth were almost inhuman. Styx held his cock so Law couldn't come until Styx allowed him to, and putting all his pleasure at Styx's disposal made everything even more intense.

He gasped as Styx bumped his prostate hard, held his cock pressed there, and then he released Law's cock. His climax spiraled out of control, made him half collapse. He reached for Paulo's hand even as Styx continued to pound him, Law's ass contracting around his cock as he pulled Styx to an orgasm with him. And he knew he never wanted these men to be done with him.

Paulo tried to picture Law and Styx as younger boys— imagined them together in the kind of frenzy that only youth could bring to sex.

When they finally collapsed and caught their breath, Paulo told them, "I can't imagine the type of heat you two generated when you were younger," because it was still off the charts.

"I think he's calling us old men again," Law said, and Styx gave a slow smile.

"I think he's due for that spanking."

Paulo tried to breathe normally, because Styx was for sure not kidding, but Law let him off the hook a little. "We fucked like rabbits when we first met," he admitted, and Styx laughed.

"Yeah, you couldn't get enough of me once I broke you in."

"Don't flatter yourself. I wasn't a virgin," Law told him.

Styx's face clouded for a brief second, until Law continued, "Dude, I don't care what your memory says— you were not a virgin at all."

That made Styx smile. "I suppose not. It was like riding a bike."

"Or being ridden." Law smirked. "My first times were crazy. In those days, it was all about club hopping and fucking as much as you could, good or bad. As long as you got off, it was all good. When I got older, my tastes got more discriminatory."

Paulo snorted and Law shook his head slowly. "You're in so much trouble, young one, you have no idea."

But he did.

"What about you?" Styx asked Paulo.

"Ah, typical teenage shit."

Law furrowed his brow a little. "Was it bad?"

"It was, ah…different." Paulo squirmed as both men looked at him, and he was trying hard to keep this secret. He wouldn't succeed. "I'm not going to be able to have any secrets around either of you, am I?"

"You don't let us have any," Law said mildly, but he was smiling as he spoke. "Spill."

"My first time was with a teacher," Paulo said, and both men simply stared at him. "I didn't know he was my teacher at the time—a sub, actually. I was sixteen and I'd snuck into a club near my house. Up until that point, I'd just messed around—guys and girls, too—but that night I was pretty determined to finally get laid."

"This oughta be good." Styx settled back for the story.

Paulo could still blush thinking about how green he'd been. How, looking back, he was sure the bouncer let him in despite his crappy fake ID, probably because Paulo had been young and blond and tight. "I downed a few shots because I was so goddamned nervous. And then this guy came over and asked me to dance. He saved me from some…" he looked between Styx and Law, "…older guys."

"So much trouble," Law muttered, and Paulo ignored that.

"He was hot, too. We danced and after about half an

hour, we ended up in the back room."

"Your first time was in a club's back room, with everyone watching?" Law asked.

Paulo nodded. There'd been something so forbidden about the whole thing that he'd had no problem getting fucked in front of other people. "The guy was decent enough—I didn't have much to judge him on for a while."

It had hurt like hell, more than he'd thought, but finally the pain had turned to something close enough to pleasure—and he'd come.

Of course, that wasn't too hard for a fifteen-year-old boy.

"So no one ever offered to spank you?" Styx asked.

"They did." Why he was admitting that was beyond him, but Law and Styx immediately perked up. There was no turning back from the story now. "I was nineteen. He was a Dom."

He'd been involved in the club scene from his first time on, always selective, always careful because of who his family was. He couldn't afford to be caught in a raid, because he was at the academy and he wanted a career in law enforcement.

"He was…" Paulo almost said older, but the two men in front of him would probably take him over their knees immediately if he made another smart comment about their age. Neither man was particularly vain, but passing thirty for a gay man was always a bit of a touchy subject… and neither Law nor Styx was immune to it. "Experienced."

Styx snorted and Law muttered, "Nice save."

"Anyway…he and I had hooked up a few times."

"Like, Dom/sub hooked up?" Law asked.

"No. Not really. Just fucking around." Literally. But the man—Dave—had always asked, would tell him he would take him over his knee and spank his ass red in front of the crowd. "That was his thing. The spanking."

"And you never took him up on it?" Styx asked.

"No." Dave had told him he could keep it private. Even had Paulo to his apartment, but in the end, Paulo wouldn't let him. "I just…couldn't."

"He's not ready." Styx spoke to Law, although he never took his eyes off Paulo. "He will be, though."

"Jesus." Paulo ran a hand through his hair and wondered how the hell he could be that embarrassed and that turned on at the same time. He recalled watching a lot of the scenes play out at Crave with interest, had jerked off thinking about a few of them but knew he could never be that on display.

"Hey, you were the one at Crave," Law pointed out.

"Yeah, looking for you."

"You sure found him," Styx said with a grin. "I'm starving. You guys hungry?"

Both men nodded and Styx slipped on a pair of jeans and went to the kitchen.

"Handy that he cooks," Paulo said, mainly because he couldn't.

"He's good to have around." Law meant it sincerely, the warmth apparent in his eyes when he looked after the man. It was still there when he looked back at Paulo, and Paulo knew it was reserved for him, too.

Fuck, this was the craziest situation ever. "Have you guys…done this before? The threesome thing?"

"Yeah, we have."

"With Damon?"

"Damon wasn't ever a part of it—wasn't even a thought. He was more into the D/s scene, even then. But Styx and I… we liked bringing a third person in, and it would be good for the night but no one ever really fit for longer than that. After Styx left, I had a few threesomes, but it was never the same. And in a weird way, it kind of solidified the fact that Styx and I belonged together."

Paulo wondered if that's what he was—a stranger they didn't want coming between them—and then he refused to believe that.

"That's not what you are," Law continued, and Paulo really wished the man would stop reading his mind. "We were young when we were doing that."

"But you liked it."

"We did. It was hot." Law paused. "I never thought it would be any kind of permanent situation. Then again, I never knew things would turn out the way they did in my life. If you'd told me I'd be going into the military when I was seventeen, even eighteen, I would've laughed in your face."

"What changed? Was it only because Styx left?"

"I don't think so. We grew up a lot in that year. Saw Greg get sicker, and we finally realized when he said that partying would only help the hurt for so long, he was right. We needed more. God knew I needed discipline, but a different kind than what I'd grown up with. It was hard as hell at first, but it was good for me—for Damon, too. We excelled. And we needed to do that."

Paulo understood. When he'd passed the test to become a New York City Police Officer, he'd done so under his mother's maiden name. From the start, none of the officers in training knew he was a son looking to follow in his father's footsteps. No, that was the last thing he wanted at first and then especially after the scandal, because his career would not take the same path his father's had and end in disgrace.

Now he knew he'd never escape that legacy, and that made him ache. Thought about all the times he'd run from something—toward an invisible something—and wondered if he'd finally be able to stop.

"You look sad." Law's voice broke through his reverie.

"I'll be all right."

"You fit with us, Paulo. You don't need to run anymore."

"We're all running," he pointed out, and Law tugged him until he was closer.

"You know what I'm saying. Maybe good is supposed to

come from bad," Law said. "What if we needed this time together to solidify us—all of us—together?"

Paulo could think of nothing more than how badly he wanted it to be that simple.

11

A few more days passed in similar fashion—lots of sex and sleep and talking, and Paulo was beginning to think that Law was right about a bad situation bringing about something good.

The cabin had begun to feel like home and maybe it was some kind of Stockholm syndrome—without the kidnapping thing. But there was an underlying tension between Law and Styx, as if Law knew Styx was planning on leaving them to finish things with his father. He couldn't hide with them forever—he had a job to do as an agent and sitting here with them wasn't getting it done.

Then again, Paulo and Law didn't plan on hiding forever, either. But until they discussed it openly, Paulo would dance around the subject as well.

God, there was so much up in the air…and if the sex wasn't there to distract them, they'd probably kill one another.

Paulo hadn't slept much the night before and he'd just started to nod off on the couch next to Law when Styx's cell rang.

"It's Tomcat," Styx said, and they all tensed and didn't bother to hide it. Normally, Tomcat's calls were simply to tell them that everything was status quo, but that could change at any time. And although the men were relaxed, they were always ready to fight for their lives. They switched up guard duty at night. They checked the grounds during the day.

And they never, ever forgot the kind of man they were dealing with.

Styx paced into the kitchen, the way he always did when Tomcat called. Paulo and Law remained on the couch as Law flipped through the channels until he found a movie he liked.

"Paulo, Tomcat needs to talk to you," Styx called. "Something about your captain demanding to know when you'd be back."

Law glanced at him. "Are you giving notice?"

"I don't think I have a choice."

"There's always a choice," Law told him.

"If it means keeping you out of trouble, then I'm choosing to resign. How's that?"

Before Law could answer, Styx came into the room. Paulo got off the couch, took the phone from him, and Styx took his place next to Law.

Paulo spoke before Law could try to persuade him not to resign. "Hey, it's Paulo. I've already got a resignation letter written."

"Keep talking about that and get someplace where Law and Styx can't hear or see you," Tomcat instructed and Paulo did, telling him some bullshit and managing to sound completely normal until he got to the front room.

If Tomcat wanted him to keep something from the other men, it had to be serious, which really worried Paulo. "I'm good—tell me what's wrong."

Tomcat was nothing if not a straight shooter. "Styx's father contacted yours. Threatened the hell out of him and the rest of your family."

Paulo's blood chilled. "Why? What's the point of that?"

"To scare your family. To draw you out."

"Fuck."

"Yep, that's what I said."

"How do they know I killed two of their men?"

Tomcat hesitated for a moment and then, "I'm thinking Styx's father was watching us at the restaurant. As for the second man, it doesn't matter. But you have family who can be threatened—Styx and Law only have each other and so you make the better bet. He's hoping you're the weak link. The one who'll break."

"What do they want?"

"To turn yourself in to them. You're supposed to meet these guys to give them intel on Styx. What do you want to do? We've put protection on your family for now, but your father's not happy."

"I'll do it, but not for my family. I'll meet with them—

and then I'll kill them," Paulo said, hearing the deadly tone to his own voice.

"Pretty much what I thought you'd say. I'll help you with the kill part, but you've got to help me figure a way to get you out of there without making the other two suspicious," Tomcat said. "Styx would have my balls for this."

"Then why are you doing it?"

"Because you can handle it. Because I think it's our best shot at getting Styx's father."

Paulo glanced toward the living room, but the men had moved into the bedroom, which was good—bought him some time. "I can do this."

It would rip his heart out to leave them, but he could.

"I'll pick you up in the morning. Around ten or so."

"I'm going to insist Styx call you in the morning, then—tell him I want out."

"Gonna let me in on the plan?"

"I'll take care of it," Paulo said, but the pain came through in his voice.

"Ah, okay…you're gonna break their hearts. Well, hell, eventually they'll get it."

"I hope so," Paulo said, the unspoken hanging between them. For all his bravado, it could be the last night he spent with the men.

There was another pause and then Tomcat admitted, "Styx's father put a hit out on him this time."

The breath caught in Paulo's throat. "What?"

"I didn't think he'd tell you."

"He said that his father wants him back."

"If that were true, I'd be calling him now instead of you. I think we can work with this. I'd asked Law to help as well, because there was no one better during his Delta days, but Styx would get too suspicious."

"I'll do it," Paulo assured him, and he and Tomcat talked for a little longer before they hung up. Paulo stuck his hands in his pockets and remained in place for a few minutes, letting the enormity of what he needed to do wash over him. The fact that Styx's father had placed the hit on Styx this time meant those shots at the first safe house weren't for Law.

For Styx to carry all of this around and not tell them… well, it made sense as to why Tomcat wanted Styx to hide with them. Styx wasn't only there for protection—he was being protected as well.

Law had watched Paulo leave the room with the phone pressed to his ear and cursed silently. Wished the man didn't have to resign—for any reason—and then he got up and moved toward the bedroom.

He was so goddamned restless—he'd been that way all day although he'd done his best to hide it and not worry Paulo—but it was the kind of thing that a good fucking would only half cure.

He hadn't needed something this badly since…shit, since forever. If this need came up, he could usually tamp it down. The few times he attempted to get what he needed, he'd asked Damon to set him up with a Dom. And while Damon's choices were always good and did everything in their power to make Law comfortable with them, he'd never been able to let himself go that way he wanted to.

But Styx would notice the agitation, if he hadn't already. No doubt he was waiting for Law to approach him, but if Law didn't, Styx would simply take over. His instincts were so finely honed to everything that Law both envied and pitied him.

The man was never off. Although now Law understood why.

He looked out the window, hadn't realized his fists were balled in his pockets, hadn't realized he'd let the frustration level climb, despite all the release he'd had. And Styx was behind him, nipping his shoulder, the back of his neck. Pressing his body against Law's.

Styx knew what he needed—the man always did. And while Law had been reluctant to ask for it—and Styx no doubt reluctant to push—when left alone, Styx didn't hesitate.

Talking to Paulo about spanking earlier had made Law squirm—both with anticipation and a sliver of fear. He didn't ask for it often, but for him, it was the best kind of relief.

Now, Styx ran a hand along his shoulders, his slightly callused palms rubbing, and then his fingers kneaded. "It's okay to ask. It's okay not to ask."

"After all these years, you still know."

"Yeah. You haven't changed all that much, Law, and I mean that as a compliment."

"You haven't either, even though you think you have."

Styx bowed his head and for a long moment, they remained like that. And then Styx lifted his head and told him, "Strip. Then get on your hands and knees on the bed."

Law swallowed hard, but after a few seconds of hesitation, he did what was asked. Took his shirt and jeans off and left them on the floor. The walk to the bed seemed to take forever although it was only a few feet. His skin tingled, his breath came fast, and he wasn't sure he'd be able to hold still.

But he tried.

Styx approached, rubbed his back, spoke to him softly, like he was some kind of wounded animal and fuck it all, in so many ways, he was.

"Spread your legs, Law. Wider." Styx got off the bed, stood over him as he tried his best not to tremble. "Good, that's good. Head down."

At Styx's words alone, Law could come. The command in his voice was something he craved and even though being submissive wasn't something he wanted long-term, when he needed it, he really needed it.

The first smacks came hard and fast, right and left cheek, and then there was a pause. He heard himself whimper and it would be really easy to turn over, to leave the room, to not need this right now.

But oh, how he did. And when Styx paused to check if he was all right, he heard himself beg roughly, "I need more, Styx…please…"

And Styx gave it to him, forced him to stay still while the smacks came and sent him where he needed to be, with no break in between, no light touch, just the hard, fast whacks of pain that made him curse and moan.

When he came, it was with a white hot, blinding light, his orgasm causing his entire body to spasm, taking with it the stress of the past days completely. The release was incredible. Necessary.

He half collapsed and Styx helped him all the way down, held him tight, whispered to him and Law didn't even have the strength to cry.

No, he didn't need to.

Paulo didn't want to make Styx or Law suspicious by lingering and trying to put on his best poker face. Luckily, judging from the sounds he heard from the back bedroom, neither man was paying his call much mind at the moment.

He walked toward it and paused a few feet away. Through the open doorway, he saw Law on his hands and knees on the bed in the hottest fucking display he'd ever seen, with Styx's hand coming down on Law's bare ass...and Law howling in pleasure.

He wasn't tied down and that made it even more intense. Styx didn't need to bind Law—he just used words and Law was still as he could be, muscles bulging, breath coming fast.

Watching Law submit to Styx was a turn-on, but this was beyond. And when Law finally came, the orgasm going on for what seemed like forever, Paulo knew why he'd been so intrigued by this kind of play.

It was the kind of release Paulo needed right now—what he'd craved and never knew. But Law and Styx both had, and how both men knew what he needed amazed him.

And tomorrow, he'd leave them, safe in the knowledge that he'd done the right thing.

He hovered near the open door, not wanting to intrude because the moment they were having was obviously emotional, but Styx had noticed him already. Law shifted and saw Paulo, and his cheeks reddened.

He looked away, like he wasn't sure how Paulo would take what he'd just seen, so Paulo came forward and touched the man's shoulder. "Should I be embarrassed to want that?"

"No," Law said, his voice hoarse.

"Then why should you be?"

"Because I like control. I've shown you that need."

"We'll work on that," Styx told them both. "But there's some other business first."

Styx was staring at Paulo when he spoke and Paulo tensed, because he knew what the man was talking about. And the thought of him spread over Styx's lap, unable to escape…Jesus Christ, he almost came in his pants.

He also wanted to get the hell out of there, but it was like Law knew that. And it was Law's turn to comfort Paulo, and he did by putting a hand on his thigh and rubbing. "Don't worry, Paulo…you're going to love it."

Paulo couldn't choke out any words, couldn't take his eyes off Styx, who got off the bed and walked over to a chair in the corner of the room.

"What did I tell you I'd do?" he asked, his voice predatory, matching the look in his eyes, and Paulo had to fight not to take a step backwards.

He opened his mouth to say no, to tell Styx to back off, but what came out was totally different. "You want to put me over your knee."

"Yeah, I do. You deserve it for that smart mouth. And I know you want it." Styx sat with his thighs parted, heavy sex jutting up.

Paulo swallowed hard, because he did. Had, from the moment Law mentioned it, and there was no more denying it.

All he could do was nod.

"Good boy. Then come on over." Styx rubbed his thighs with his palms but it was like Paulo was stuck to the floor. Tried to envision what it would be like, what it would feel like, and found himself shivering a little. Wanting it, but unable to move toward it, like so many other things he'd let slip by in his life.

But these men wouldn't let him skate away—not that easily…not at all.

"I'll come get you, Paulo, if that's what it takes." Styx didn't bother to wait for an answer. He got up and closed the gap between them, pulled Paulo in for a deep kiss first and Paulo was grateful, because it helped him to relax. Styx's hands were in his hair, running along his back, gripping his ass and somehow they were walking and kissing without falling, in the general direction of the chair.

But Paulo pulled back. "Will you stop if I need you to?"

"I don't play like that," Styx told him. "These are my rules. You can handle it."

"What if I don't?" Paulo asked and Styx gave him a half smile.

"You'll come, Paulo. And you'll come apart—that's the goal. And you will handle it—how you do, well, that's up to you."

Styx sat in the chair then, and Paulo remained standing next to him until Styx tugged him to a kneeling position. He'd been naked in front of Styx for days now, it seemed, but he'd never felt more naked or vulnerable than he did at this moment, kneeling in front of Styx.

From where he knelt, Paulo had a close up view of Styx's cock. Couldn't help but lean in and use his mouth to make a slow up-and-down drag over it, spinning the piercing slightly with his tongue.

Above him, he heard Styx groan, "You little shit," and he smiled with his mouth full of cock and did it again and again until Styx was holding his head in place, thrusting his hips up to fuck Paulo's mouth.

The air in the room changed, and Paulo could feel Law's eyes on him.

"You're not getting out of it," Styx told him after he opened his eyes. Paulo looked up at him and across the room at Law, who sat at the edge of the bed, jerking his own cock.

"Definitely not," Law breathed.

Styx urged Paulo to lie across his lap so his hard cock pressed Styx's thighs, and holy shit, the friction would kill him instantly. Fear gripped him hard as he tried to close his eyes and wait for the first strike of Styx's hand, but the struggle inside him wasn't waning.

It was growing stronger. "Styx, I can't," he whispered.

But Styx's only answer was to hold him fast and then bring down a palm on his bare ass. The sharp crack reverberated in the room, inside his mind, and he knew he was lost.

The next two came down in rapid succession and he still

fought because it was humiliating and hot and necessary. Because he knew there was nothing he could do to stop it…had to lie here and take everything Styx gave him.

Because it had never felt so right and still, he heard himself beg Styx to let him go before things went too far.

Styx had paused after a few slaps, watching to see if Paulo would sink deep into the submission, or if he'd need more.

"Do it," Law practically whispered, his voice raw. Watching Styx balance Paulo over his knee as the younger man squirmed with embarrassment and impatience and fear…and arousal as well, was making him want to throw himself on Styx's mercy again.

Styx had a way of taking away all the pain and hurt with a few strokes. He would've made a good Dom but never had any interest beyond doing his own thing with Law. And now, with Paulo.

"Let me go, dammit." Paulo was really struggling, until Styx brought a bare hand down on his ass a few more times and then he stiffened and went strangely silent.

Law had seen it happen before, mainly between Damon and the men who wanted to sub for him. The art of surrendering, of submitting, could be a beautiful thing if done well…and Styx always had the right touch.

Again, Styx's hand met Paulo's bare skin—then twice

more with hard smacks that rang through the air that was thick with tension and lust. Paulo moaned then, a low, keening sound, and Law had never heard anything more beautiful. And Styx continued his assault, not letting up as Paulo's ass reddened and he squirmed against Styx's thighs, a sure sign he was enjoying himself.

But the younger man was still unsure, whimpered a little when Styx took a break and Styx looked up at Law with a question in his eyes.

"He can handle it, Styx. Give him more."

At Law's words, Paulo's protests began again in earnest until the hard, steady slaps wouldn't allow for any further resistance. Law watched it all drain from Paulo's muscles as he became pliant and wanton under the blows and finally, he let it all go, his orgasm taking him by complete surprise.

When Styx helped him off his lap, Paulo ended up kneeling on the floor by Styx's thighs again, rested a forehead on Styx's knee while he composed himself. And then, just as Law knew they would, the tears came and Styx was on the floor next to Paulo, holding him, telling him how damned good he was.

Although Styx had no desire to be a Dom, Damon had always told him he was a natural. The way both Paulo and Law responded to him was evidence enough, and if that was what these men needed from time to time, Styx was more than happy to give them their pleasure.

Paulo fell apart in his arms, like he knew the younger man would, which made Law nearly lose it again. So Styx comforted both men, and when Paulo calmed down, Styx rubbed lotion on his ass then drew the sheet up over him. Law was next to him, and he wrapped himself around Paulo, the two men murmuring quietly to one another when Styx went to make them something to eat.

If you'd asked him a month ago if he thought he'd be fucking Law—and Law's almost-boyfriend—he would've never believed it. But now being with both men seemed as natural as breathing.

And how it would all end was something he refused to think about now. It would bring the tension back to his shoulders and since he'd gotten off several times while getting Law and Paulo off, he wanted to remain in this semi-blissful state for a bit longer.

He brought in the sandwiches and sodas. Paulo was quiet, his eyes red-rimmed, and he was still half lost in space but he ate and drank, as did Law. The three men lay there as fresh snow drifted around the house.

Neither Paulo nor Law had been outside in days, since the firewood was stored in the garage. Styx still went to check to make sure no one had driven or walked up close to the house, and in this snow, footprints and tire tracks would be a dead giveaway.

Paulo was more restless than he should've been after the spanking, which worried Styx. He didn't want to quiz the younger man, since he'd turned away and closed himself off a bit, even though his gut told him to.

But Law shook his head, like he knew what Styx was thinking, and so against his better judgment he let both men drift off to sleep while he stayed awake to watch over them, the way he'd done so many nights before.

12

In the middle of the night, Paulo rolled off the bed and went to the bathroom to piss. He stared at himself in the mirror, saw the conflict in his eyes and wanted nothing more than to crawl back into bed with the two men he'd left.

Styx hadn't actually been sleeping—most nights he stayed up with Law and stood guard, the familiar tin box of Altoids never far from his side. The man went through them like crazy. Paulo didn't have their stamina for non-sleep—or their insomnia problem—and they never made him feel guilty about it.

But fuck, the guilt washed over him now.

You have to do this for them. And now was as good a time as any. He didn't rejoin the men, instead moving to the couch and wrapping a blanket around himself.

After half an hour, Law came to check on him.

"You all right?"

"I want to be alone," he said curtly, and the silence was like a cold wall slamming between them.

"Okay." Law didn't walk away though.

"Didn't you hear me?"

"I did." Law paused. "Is this about what happened earlier? Because sometimes—"

"Stop, Law." God, he hated this, hated to have either man think that they'd pushed him away because of the spanking, but it seemed the most reasonable excuse, given his earlier freak-outs when it had been mentioned. It was completely plausible that he'd be having second thoughts about what had actually happened, and he was banking on that for his escape. "I need to be alone."

"Paulo, please, let's talk about it. It can be freaky at first."

Paulo put his head down and said, "Fuck off. I'm tired of talking about all of it."

Law remained in place behind him for a few moments longer. Finally, he heard footsteps and muffled voices and then no one came back, which was good. They probably figured giving him what he asked for tonight and would want to talk more about it in the morning.

The hours dragged by and finally, Styx came into the room. "Paulo—"

"I want to talk to Tomcat."

Styx sighed. "Can we talk first?"

"No. I need to get the hell out of here. I'm not a prisoner, am I?"

"No, you're not. You never were."

Paulo couldn't turn around to look at him, because if

his eyes were as sad as his words… "Good, then please call him."

"I will. But I'm sorry—we didn't mean to push you too hard."

Paulo couldn't turn around—his throat was tight with the lie. Because he'd fucking loved it—every second, and how could Styx not see that reflected in his eyes?

Because being a damned good liar right now will save their lives.

And that thought was enough to force him to push forward.

Paulo didn't look back. Law knew, because he'd watched him from the opened garage until he couldn't see the truck in the distance any longer.

Styx tugged him back in and closed the garage door—safety reasons, but it still killed Law. For a long moment he remained rooted to the spot as if he could see through the metal, as if the truck would come roaring back down the road with Paulo realizing he'd made a mistake.

Finally, he turned and went into the house where Styx was making coffee in the kitchen. Styx pushed a cup at him and Law drank it absently—it was strong, but Styx had lightened it for him with milk and sugar, the way Law liked it.

"I can't believe," Law started then stopped, his throat suddenly too tight. He swallowed a few times, then took a deep breath. "How did I read him so wrong?"

"I think he got scared."

Whatever freaked Paulo out happened in the middle of the night—or else it was something he'd started thinking of earlier. "The spanking? Too intense?"

"Maybe. He seemed okay afterwards, but sometimes, if you think about it too much…" Styx trailed off and Law tried to remember the first time Styx had done it to him.

Having come from a violent background, he'd been surprised that the act itself hadn't triggered more of a reaction. But it had been cathartic, and putting himself under Styx's hand, trusting him completely, had been more of a relief than anything.

But for Paulo… "We have to get him back."

"He'll come back to us. He has to." Styx poured himself more coffee and Law knew the man hadn't been sleeping well at all. Law found him by the window most nights, gun in hand as if waiting for the worst.

"And then what?" Law heard himself ask, and Styx didn't say anything for a long moment, just drank his coffee and stared out the window.

When he did speak, they were words that Law was happy to hear.

"There's a connection there, a powerful one I can't deny."

Law had felt it with Paulo from the start, which was why

he'd fought so hard to keep the detective away from him.

Little fucker was really persistent. And easy to talk to, plus had an uncanny awareness of what Law did and didn't need.

"He's gorgeous," Styx continued. "At first, I thought it was that…and the fact that he had you and I was jealous as hell for that."

Paulo was a handsome man—nothing feminine about him, which had never attracted either Law or Styx. Both liked their men on the rugged side and Paulo had everything…the face, the tats… Just thinking about Paulo made Law hard, and Styx noticed when he shifted at his arousal.

"That's for him."

"Plenty to go around." Law paused. "We used to share all the time."

"It never worked out well. We always ended up fucking and ignoring the third person. But that hasn't happened here."

"Because this time, there's way more to it than simple sharing." Styx stared at him like he had three heads, a really apropos sentiment, Law mused wryly. "He's us. Lost. Stubborn. Strong. He needs us the same way we need him."

"I want him. I still want more of him. And that really doesn't bother you?"

Law smiled. "No. It was just what I was hoping for, actually."

"What the hell are we going to do? What happens from here?"

"We get Paulo and bring him home with us," Law said.

"He's not going to be convinced easily."

"Yeah well, we probably wouldn't have it any other way. But it would've been easier if we hadn't let him go in the first place."

"We had to let him go. He's not a prisoner, and the best way to make him realize what he was walking away from was to let him walk. Tomcat will make sure he's safe."

Law softened at that. "You really do want him back."

"Yeah. Even though I think this whole thing is crazy." Styx shook his head. "I'm going to have to leave soon to deal with this. I keep telling you and you keep saying no but…"

"Forget it. We find Paulo, bring him back and then we deal with this together."

"Damon must like him."

"He does." Law paused. "I still can't believe he's in love. Content. Finally."

Styx raised his brows. "I know he lost someone a little while back."

"Yes, and then someone else walked in." The road for Tanner and Damon hadn't been easy, wouldn't be as long as Tanner served, but Law had faith in them. The one thing that they'd all feared was that life was too short not to spend as much time with the one you loved as possible.

"I'm sorry I didn't come when you called."

"I didn't ask you to."

"Not in so many words, no."

He'd given Styx his final version of goodbye, had cut the lines of communication once and for all, and then he'd been attacked by a man from their past.

Now, to find out that Styx had been at the hospital that night, checking to make sure he was okay… "Why didn't you let me know you were there that night in the hospital?"

"I wanted to. I would've, but then I saw him—Paulo—with you. The way he looked at you…the way you looked at him. You pushed him away and that's when I knew."

"Knew what?"

"That you felt something for him." Styx paused. "Don't you remember, you tried the same thing with me in the beginning too? It wasn't all love at first sight—at least not for you."

It had been—Law had been too stubborn to admit it. He thought back to when Styx first entered his life—he'd been cocky as hell to hide the fear, but with Styx, it had been different right from the start.

Law had been alone with Greg—healing—for a year before he brought Styx home. It had been a complete surprise, unlike when Damon came to live with them. Damon had been sleeping on the cot in the back room of Greg's club for a bit, and Law knew it was only a matter of time before Greg opened his home to him.

It hadn't been bad. Damon was fucked up but he stayed out of Law's way, let Law get to know him.

But when Styx came in first, the man had just invaded. He was rude and nosy and unrelenting. A cocky asshole.

"You hated me," Styx reminded him.

Law smiled at the truth of those words. "You drove me fucking nuts."

"I wanted to get close to you…wanted to crawl inside and never come out," Styx told him, and sometime after the first two months, the men had a knock-down, drag-out fight that ended in them kissing.

"Bullshit—you have no memory," Law told him, and the look that crossed Styx's face was one of such true pain that Law wanted to take his words back, but it was too late.

He went to pull away but Law jerked him back on top of him, held him tight.

"Sorry, Styx…so fucking sorry," he murmured into Styx's neck. Wanted to heal him…to fuck him, to open himself like he never had before.

And then Styx was moving against him—his cock had been hard, Law assumed, because of the fight, the adrenaline, but he finally realized there was more to it.

"Wanted you from the day I moved in," Styx told him, and Law knew it to be true when Styx kissed him.

"That was a good night," Law said, and Styx rumbled from somewhere deep in his chest at the memory.

"Do we have more left?"

"You know I do. Do I have to promise you?"

"Yeah—promise that you won't get so roped up on revenge that you won't come back," Law told him.

It was settling in that they were alone…and for the first time they'd have to face their demons and make peace with nothing to distract them. He didn't protest when Styx picked him up and put him on the counter, ripping his sweats down so he was bare-assed on the cold granite, Styx's cock rubbing his. Law cradled Styx's head as the man sucked his nipple hard.

"Yeah, that's it, Styx… You can make me come like that…"

That seemed to be Styx's objective as he tongued the nipple and used his fingers on the other one, and Law rubbed against him like a goddamned cat in heat. He buried his face in Styx's hair, the man's scent an aphrodisiac, his tongue working magic against the already tender nubs, and how the hell did he always know what Law needed and when?

His cock dripped precome and his balls tightened.

"Wrap around me," Styx instructed, and Law did, so his ass was mostly off the counter and Styx bore most of his weight. But he stopped himself before he came, murmured, "I want to fuck you," and felt Styx's body stiffen against him.

It had only happened twice before. Once, when they were younger and living at Greg's and the next, on Styx's final visit to Law's apartment when he was still in Delta

Force and home on leave.

He'd come in from a four-month long mission and found Styx in his bed, waiting for him. They didn't talk for hours and when Law woke that next morning, Styx was long gone.

Now, he waited for Styx's reaction. Styx didn't like to bottom at all—it just wasn't his thing. But if Law remembered correctly, the man had been begging for more those two times—he just didn't like to admit it.

"Come on, Law," he started to protest, but Law stopped him.

"I'm sore as hell from you."

"So I'll suck your cock instead, baby."

"No dice. Let me in. All the way." He'd spoke those words recently to Paulo as well, and the man had trusted him enough to do so. "I'll make it good—you know that."

Styx conceded, but not with words. Instead, he put Law back on the counter and dropped his pants, then turned and held onto the counter.

And if he wanted it this Spartan, Law would give him exactly what he wanted. He took the lube and used it on his fingers, began to stroke Styx's ass.

"Don't treat me like a fucking virgin," Styx growled, and Law inserted a finger inside and then a second. Styx groaned and dropped his head.

He was tight as anything—his breathing was a little harsh, too—and for a second, Law almost stopped.

"Let me make it good for you," he whispered as his fingers probed Styx, scissoring, opening him up. Readying him.

He would've loved to tongue the man's ass, but Styx wouldn't wait for him to do that, would want it rough and tumble, and he would oblige the man.

He started slowly, until the head of his cock breached Styx, and then he pushed all the way in, nearly taking Styx off the floor and only then did he hear a low, keening moan. He took Styx's hips and pistoned in and out, because if memory served, Styx liked this part rough, hated being babied in any way, shape or form. And Styx yelled Law's name as he clutched the counter with one hand and his cock with the other, and then Law bent his head and bit Styx on the side of the neck as he came.

Styx came seconds later, barely able to hold on, and if it wasn't for Law they would've tumbled to the floor.

"Fuck me," Styx breathed, and Law laughed.

"Didn't think you'd be up for it again that fast."

"Don't even try it." Styx turned—his face was flushed, and he gathered Law against him. "It's your turn, because if I don't fuck you to sleep, you'll never get any shut-eye."

It was true—and Law knew he'd be too full of worry for Paulo no matter what, but that didn't mean he wouldn't let Styx try his best.

Paulo was wired for sound, knew Tomcat was backing him up. The plan was in place. Tomcat told the usual suspects at the CIA where Paulo's new safe house was.

Just like the first time, they were counting on a leak. This time Tomcat could concentrate on finding out who it was based on how he disseminated the intel, and Paulo hoped Styx's father would send in men he could trail, if not come himself.

Tomcat hadn't told a soul about Law and Styx's location at the old cabin and Paulo was content in the knowledge that those men were safely hidden away.

Now, he would take steps to ensure they stayed that way.

He remained pressed to the ground under the house and waited for the men to show. There would be two this time—Tomcat was sure they would know to bring backup after what had happened to the last assassin.

The men knew they were up against cops, agents and Delta Force. They wouldn't take chances.

Paulo could slide easily out of his hiding spot. Once the men entered the house looking for him, he'd put the tracking device on their car. Follow them back to the city.

This time, there was less stealth on their part. They rolled up to the house where Paulo had left the TV on and some lights, a coffeepot that was still warm. The men would find tire tracks going down the old road and assume he'd heard them and ran.

It would barely give Paulo enough time to do what he needed to, but he was ready.

Once they went in, he snaked across the front lawn in the dark, placed the tracker under the front tire of their car and snuck into the woods instead of risking the walk back to the house.

He lay in wait, closer to the men than he'd been before, pistol pulled in case he'd been made. When the men walked back to their car, it was apparent they were angry.

"Fossman got the intel right, but the guy made us," the shorter of the two was telling someone on the other end of his cell phone. "We're going after him now to see if we can pick up his trail."

Paulo used the light from the car's interior to catch a glimpse of his features—he looked nothing like Styx but still he committed the face to memory so he could describe it to a sketch artist if necessary or look through some CIA wanted pics. He couldn't see the other guy worth a damn.

At least they knew Fossman was the leak.

He forced his breathing to calm until they drove away, didn't stay put because he had a feeling they'd circle back around to check the house again. He threaded his way back through the woods to meet Tomcat at the end of the hidden road.

The hunter's instincts Paulo's father had always prided

himself on his son having were even stronger now, despite missing buck season for at least eight years. It was something he'd used to try to bond with his father, whose cop instincts had always known there was something different about Paulo.

"You're a queer, aren't you?" he'd sneered one day up at the old cabin.

"No one uses queer anymore," Paulo told him calmly, waited to eat the back of his father's hand, but the shot never came.

His father was scared to touch him as though being gay was a communicable disease.

To Paulo's father, it was. And that had been the last hunting trip.

Three weeks later, his father had been arrested for prisoner abuse and Paulo's world turned inside out.

It was that way again, and he'd begun to doubt whether he'd ever feel completely safe anyplace again.

He spotted Tomcat's truck and headed toward it, allowed himself to think briefly on Law and Styx…and then cursed himself for doing so.

Fuck, he missed them, and it had only been three goddamned days.

Maybe they missed him too, or maybe they'd begun to realize that the three of them together wasn't necessary, that Paulo had simply been a way to facilitate their reconnecting.

Thinking about that made his heart pound unnaturally.

He stopped, put his hand against a tree trunk, needing to pull himself together before he got into the truck with Tomcat.

What had he expected? He'd known Law for less than six months, had been on a couple of dates that were little more than fucking sessions.

Just because he'd fallen in love didn't mean Law had. And the fact that he'd been the only one to use the word love in the past weeks hadn't been lost on him—it just hit him with more force now since he'd left.

He'd known Styx for only a few days and felt more of an attachment to him than he had with men he'd been lovers with for a year.

There was definitely something fucked up about him. At twenty-eight, he wasn't supposed to be having this love-at-first-sight bullshit happening to him. That should've happened when he was a teen, but at that point, he'd been too busy dealing with the fallout from his family after coming out to them—bringing a lover into that environment wouldn't have worked at all.

And now he was alone again.

You saved him. You gave him and Styx their second chance. And hell, those two deserved it. He'd only had to be around them for a few minutes to feel the electricity between them.

He pushed off the tree, shoving the pity party down, and walked to the truck.

"You okay?" Tomcat asked when he got in, and Paulo didn't bother to lie.

"Just took a trip down memory lane I shouldn't have."

"Stop letting your past fuck with you," Tomcat admonished, like it was that simple. And maybe it was—maybe that was the key.

"Are they transmitting?" Paulo asked.

Tomcat pointed to the red star on the GPS mounted to his dash as he drove away down another back road. "Don't want to spook the spooks, so we'll let them get an hour ahead." In the meantime, the men lay low at a local diner, with Tomcat's truck hidden among the semis in the back lot.

"They're worried," Tomcat told Paulo finally, and Paulo had known it was only a matter of time before he brought up Law and Styx.

"You said you wouldn't go there."

"I lied. I do it professionally." Tomcat stared at him innocently, like that was a complete justification.

"Don't you have a love life of your own to worry about?"

"Yeah, I do." Tomcat's face clouded briefly, and because he could see that Tomcat was suffering too, it made it easier to talk.

"They're together. That's the way it should've been from the start."

"They want you back."

"How's that supposed to work?"

"Don't know. I can barely handle a non-relationship with one man." Tomcat checked the time and called to the waitress for more coffee to go. "I'll take care of the leak personally."

"Can we use him to track Styx's father?"

Tomcat slid him a glance. "Didn't realize you were CIA."

"I'm a cop—that's better."

"You sure you're up for what comes next?"

Paulo had been training for this—ready for it—his entire life. He just hadn't known he'd be doing it for two men he loved. "More than. For Styx and Law."

"For Styx and Law," Tomcat repeated. "Let's go over the plan again—I want you to eat, sleep and breathe it."

13

Paulo surrendered himself to the two hit men he'd seen at the safe house two days earlier. He forced himself to remain calm as they put a bag over his head and dragged him inside a warehouse, hoped Tomcat had been able to get through the steel doors before they locked again.

There was no way out now, not without Tomcat's help.

He'd wanted to be dragged in front of Styx's father, but that wasn't going to happen. He figured these men would never talk during an interrogation, but maybe they'd flip on one another.

All Paulo knew was that he had to stay alive long enough for Tomcat to gather the intel they needed to take things to the next level.

He thought about what Law had told him about his Delta training after they'd watched a war movie together, about how torture was so effective not because of the actual pain—although that was a bitch—but because the threat of the unknown, of what your captors could do to you, was ever present.

"It'll fuck with your mind if you let it," Law told him. "Best to stay in the present."

It had made so much sense when Law said it, more so now as Paulo remained tied to a chair, attempting to interrogate the men threatening to end his life.

"I want to see your boss," Paulo said through gritted teeth once they pulled the hood off him. He blinked a few times, because the room was bright and the sudden light hurt his eyes. He'd been tied to a chair and it was the only furniture in this room. Beyond it was an open door that led to a smaller room with a desk and an opened laptop, and he hoped that would contain the intel they needed.

"He doesn't want to see you," one of the men spat at him. "But your family's worried."

Yeah, that was bullshit. But Paulo clenched his jaw as if their words angered him.

"You tell us where Styx is, and maybe your family won't be hurt. That's the deal."

"I want to hear it from your boss," Paulo said, earning a hard slap across the face with the back of a hand.

"You give me something and then I give you something."

"Last I heard, they were in the house upstate." He rattled off the address of the house the men had already searched.

"Try again—he's not there," the man growled in his face.

"Then he's probably coming for you."

Another backhanded slap and then a punch to the side of the head and he lost consciousness. When he came to, everything throbbed and he wasn't sure what was happening.

The men were standing behind him and he didn't see any sign of Tomcat, and he wondered if this whole thing had gone south.

"He's not the important one," one of the men told him, and yeah, that could stomp on his heart if he let it.

"He'll talk more, then." The second man with the green shirt pushed at Paulo, who couldn't open one swollen eye more than a slit. "Where are they?"

Paulo spit at him and laughed, which earned him a right hook. He kicked and made contact with one of them, which brought both men down on him, because he'd caught sight of Tomcat by the computer in the corner of the next room.

The chair went down, with the men concentrating on him—and if Tomcat was right, that computer would have all the possible addresses where Styx's father lived.

They needed to catch him at home, where he was most vulnerable. Everyone was most vulnerable when they were home, no matter how good their alarm system was.

He managed to get a hand free of the ropes, dug into one of the men's pockets for his cell. In the ruckus, he slipped it into his own pocket and shoved his hand behind him again, hoped the cell wouldn't ring. And then there were more men, shining lights in his face, threatening his family.

Then they started talking about Styx. "He won't show for this one. He likes the other fag."

They were talking about Law, and Paulo wanted to kick all their asses. He might've, because he didn't remember much—there was a lot of yelling and punches and grunting, and he freed himself using the sharp edge of a broken chair on the ropes holding his wrists.

And then, just like that, the fighting stopped and he was lying on the floor, dazed. Looked up to see Tomcat hovering over him.

"My pocket," he remembered telling Tomcat before he passed out.

He remembered passing out—after that, the sensation of being carried and then floating outside his body.

Must've been in the hospital then, the drugs helping the I-don't-give-a-shit feeling. He clung to that when he opened his eyes to find himself on a bed and alone in what looked like a hospital room.

Alone.

He closed his eyes again and let sleep overtake him.

"Law, come on."

Styx was shaking him hard and at first Law thought it was one of Styx's dreams. But it wasn't. He sat up and saw the worry in Styx's eyes. "What the hell?"

"It's Paulo. He's hurt."

"Shit." Law got out of bed and yanked on clothes, didn't

waste time asking questions because they'd have a long drive for that. Styx was already packing for them—handed Law a rifle and a gun, and together they left the house under the cover of darkness.

Styx drove along the old country roads, full of snow and ice, and Law tried to tamp down the panic about Paulo.

"What did Tomcat say?" he asked finally.

"Not much," Styx said grimly. "The doc's with Paulo now—apparently, he's pretty beat up."

"What happened?"

"I think he and Tomcat tried to go after my father."

"Fuck." Law took a long drink from the soda he'd grabbed on the way out. "How much longer?"

"Couple of hours. Tomcat will call with updates as soon as he gets them. But he's okay, Law. I know that."

Law did too. There was a connection there and he would've felt the loss. "He needs us."

"That's why we're headed there."

Seventy-two hours had passed since Paulo left. "How could the hit men have found him—I thought Tomcat took care of the leak?"

"He would've kept Paulo's whereabouts private either way," Styx said, his voice dark with anger. "This had to be some crazy fucking plan of Tomcat's that Paulo went along with."

It would certainly explain Paulo's shift in attitude, and it had happened after talking with Tomcat. Everything was starting to fall into place now—and Law knew there wasn't anything Paulo wouldn't do to help get them out of their dangerous situation.

"Tomcat's been good to you. Give him the benefit of the doubt, all right?" Law reminded him, then stopped the preaching because he needed to be quiet in order to hold it together. He watched the road with Styx, listened to the weather on the radio and finally, after what seemed like forever, they were in the underground hospital parking lot on level seven, where Tomcat was waiting to take them up the elevator typically reserved for staff only.

"He's going to be all right—the doc was just with him," was all Tomcat said before he ushered them into a private room on the sixth floor. It was in the corner and a guard stood inside the room for now, in front of the curtain.

It hadn't been that long ago that Law himself lay in the hospital bed in pain and pissed and scared because Paulo had come to see him.

Scared, because he knew he'd have to push the man away. Now, Law and Styx stopped short of going to the bed where Paulo lay, and Law heard Styx pull in a rough breath.

"It looks worse than it is," Tomcat told them, but his face was slightly ashen. "He's fine—you can talk to the doctor and he'll tell you."

Law chose to believe that because he needed to cling to something, and he pushed past him to get to Paulo.

He'd been worked over good—but his face bore less of

the damage than his chest. Yes, there were multiple bruises and a split lip, a knot on his forehead at his hairline, but the bruises clustered on his right side worried Law the most. He put a hand out that hovered over them as if that could heal him and oh, how he wished that were true.

"Jesus Christ," Styx whispered from the other side of the bed, his face pale.

"He'll rouse, but they've got him pretty well snowed because of the pain," Tomcat explained. "He's got to stay here for a few days and after that—"

"He comes back to the cabin with us," Styx told him and got no argument. "You going to tell us what happened?"

"Yeah, I will," Tomcat said, his voice heavy with recrimination. "It's his family—they were threatened."

"And you didn't tell me?"

"No, I didn't. This was Paulo's call to make."

"Why the hell are you trying to shield me?"

"Because someone has to," Tomcat said fiercely. "They used you the first time and you paid a hell of a price. I swore to myself if things went down with your father again, I wouldn't let you out there to hang yourself."

"So you let Paulo instead."

"The man can handle himself. You have no idea," Tomcat told him. "He took out four of your father's best men in this condition. And as soon as he wakes up, I can guarantee he'll have more intel for me."

"Why the hell would he do that? His family disowned

him. Let them go into hiding. All they're going to do is use this against him." Law was so angry at Paulo's family and even at Paulo, although he understood that Paulo's guilt about his father's prison term—and what he'd done to get there—ran too deep to shake.

"It's all wrapped up in saving us, too," Styx said quietly, and the two men held hands over Paulo as the man's breathing stayed strong and even.

"What are you not telling me?" Law's words were directed to Styx and Tomcat held up his hands and stepped back.

"My father didn't want me back this time. He wanted me dead."

"Ah, fuck." Law ran his hands through his hair and glanced back at Paulo. "Did he know that?"

"I told him," Tomcat said, and Styx took a step toward him.

"Styx, don't. He did it for your own good. And Paulo knew what he was getting into." Law put a hand on Styx's wrist. "From now on, no more goddamned secrets. This affects all our lives, including Tomcat's. So while Paulo's recovering, we'll have a war room conference here. And we'll come up with something."

Both Tomcat and Styx nodded, and Law took a breath.

"He could've told you. I left that up to him," Tomcat added.

"So that's why he picked the fight," Law murmured.

"You can't blame him for wanting to protect you," Tomcat pointed out. "Can't blame me either."

"What about the getting beat-up part? Who do I blame for that?" Styx asked, but there was no rancor for his partner.

"Part of the plan. I was there to make sure it didn't get too out of hand," Tomcat said quietly. "I didn't leave the other side of the wall. I waited until he called me—until he got what he needed. He was in control, Styx, even though what you're seeing shows something different."

Law didn't want to think about what Paulo had submitted to on purpose. "Tell me it was worth it."

"It was. I got an address, an alarm code and several other key pieces of intel because of Paulo's bravery," Tomcat said. "We're so close—we're there. It's not going to be long now before we can put this behind us. Styx's father's angry at him—and anger makes people sloppy."

Law nodded, because he agreed with that. And then he went to Paulo and took his hand, much in the same way Paulo had his when he was in the hospital a few months earlier. Leaned down, whispered, "We're here," in his ear while Styx went to the other side of the bed and smoothed the hair from Paulo's face.

He continued holding the man's hand as he told Tomcat and Styx, "We're not leaving until he does."

No one argued with him.

He fucking hated hospitals. But this time, Styx hadn't remained behind the curtain, was with the two men the way he'd wanted to be three months earlier, before he'd put them all in danger.

He forced himself to stare at Paulo's face and body. *Your fault.* And he had the strangest feeling this wasn't the first time someone he loved had been harmed by his father.

Someone he loved…

He hadn't ever thought about anyone but Law in those terms and now having those feelings about Paulo was natural.

But neither of the men here should love him—hell, they shouldn't be involved with him at all. And with that thought, he moved away from the bed and went to leave the room.

Law stopped him, though.

"He'll be all right," Law told him… Law was comforting him this time, kissing his neck, his cheek, running his hands along Styx's arms. "Come on, baby. You and I know he's stronger than that."

All Styx could do was press his face to Law's shoulder. He hadn't cried about any of this—not really—and now he knew he wouldn't be able to stop. Here at Paulo's bedside, realizing that his father nearly took away someone else from him—and wasn't planning on stopping—his resolve strengthened. "I think you should take Paulo back to the cabin—"

"No," Law said firmly. "We're together in this. This one…" he motioned to Paulo, "…isn't coming out with us when we go after the bastard."

He let the *we* part go and agreed that Paulo was sitting the next round out.

Judging by the x-rays, his ribs were merely bruised, not broken, but Styx knew they'd still hurt like hell.

While Paulo slept, he catalogued those bruises, committing them to memory so they'd know exactly how to make those men pay.

"They wanted to put him through hell," Law had whispered, and even though he'd seen far worse in his time, he still looked shattered. "I'm helping you finish this. I'm as much a part of it as you."

Styx couldn't deny that—or Law—any longer. Paulo had gone so far out on a limb, now it was their turn to finish it.

First, they would heal Paulo. And then maybe Styx could finally find a way to heal himself.

They stayed in the hospital room with Paulo, not leaving his side for four days. Tomcat himself guarded the door along with two other agents but he'd given Styx and Law a wide berth.

Finally, on the day they were taking Paulo back to the cabin, Tomcat came into the room and Styx left Law sitting by Paulo so he could set things right with Tomcat.

He'd forgiven his partner for the most part—Tomcat had stood by him when most men wouldn't have. After all, he'd been saddled with Styx when he was young and pissed at the world—and had a target on his back.

Styx found out later that Tomcat had requested to be partnered with him.

"I knew you were loyal," he'd explain later, and yes, that was one quality Styx had in spades.

Tomcat was thirty-six a tall-assed motherfucker with a penchant for men and women—sometimes at the same time—and Styx loved the hell out of him.

"You all kiss and make up?" Tomcat asked.

"Literally, yes."

Tomcat smiled. "Well hell, Styx, I didn't think you were that kinky."

"Me neither."

"What about me? You still pissed?"

"Yes."

Tomcat took a slug of his coffee. "Paulo's got a future with the agency. They don't give a fuck that his old man's a bigoted asshole."

"I think that's a requirement."

That made Tomcat snort quietly—Styx knew he'd had a shitty childhood as well. Everyone in the agency who worked ops seemed to—some kind of issue with gaining control and never wanting to let it go. "True, that."

Tomcat hailed from Louisiana—had some Cajun blood and some blue blood, and he still spoke with that low sweet drawl. "Am I losing a partner?" he asked now as Styx glanced back at Paulo and Law.

"Ah Christ, I'm not making any decisions until this is over."

"It will be. And then you've got some nice ass to go home to." Tomcat took another swig of coffee. His dark hair was tied back at the neck, kept long because of the op, but he wore more of a rocker goatee than a long scraggily beard. Dressed in all black—and with the jacket that bore the rocker of the motorcycle gang thrown into the backseat of his truck, he could easily pass for a rock star.

"What about you? I'm sure you're getting plenty of ass."

Tomcat smiled a little, but it wasn't the wide-open smirk Styx had been expecting. "Holy fuck, don't tell me you fell for someone in the middle of an op."

"Yeah, because that would be wrong, and you're leading by example."

"Who is she? Or he?"

Tomcat gave him a sideways look. "He's young."

"Good luck with that. Try not to get arrested."

"Not that young. He's Special Forces. Twenty-five. It's too crazy to even think about."

"Why's that?"

"Because he made me within an hour after sleeping with me. Nearly a year and a half—before this, how many missions and no one's ever made me."

"You think he'd tell anyone?"

"No way. He gets it." Tomcat shook his head and then added, "He gets it a little too well."

"What did he say?"

"He whispered, 'I'd say FBI but I'll bet you'd be insulted.' And then he sucked my dick and I didn't care."

Styx shook his head and wondered what the hell was in the water these days.

He was high on pain meds and everything still goddamned hurt. And although he wasn't sure where the hell he was, he was pretty sure he was alone.

Fuck.

"Paulo."

Law's voice. Law, on the bed with him. "I'm here."

"Good for you," he managed.

"Someone needs more happy pills."

That was Styx. The men were lying on either side of him, making him the meat in this particular sandwich. He didn't hear Tomcat and he wondered what Law and Styx knew about what had happened to him.

Then the pain made him not care all that much. He must've winced or groaned because Law was urging him, "Come on, take your pill."

Paulo shook his head, and that's when Law sucked his cock and Paulo's jaw dropped and Styx put the pill in.

"Drink—don't spit it out," Styx admonished as Law sucked harder. Paulo did what he asked because he did not want that one sensation of pleasure to end.

He came fairly quickly, and while the orgasm was muted, it still made him able to drift back to sleep, but not before he heard Styx say, "Wait till the sponge bath."

When he woke again, he was in the same place on the bed, the men were still with him, watching TV, and it was dark in the room. His head was still murky, but better than it had been earlier.

"Hey." Law stroked his hair and Styx straightened the blankets.

"Where am I?"

"The cabin. You were in the hospital for four days but we didn't want to risk more time so exposed like that," Law explained.

"You guys came to the hospital?"

"We were both there," Law said. "Nothing could've kept us away."

Paulo closed his eyes as his head began to throb, and he felt like he was drifting off again. He didn't want that, needed to be on alert. "You're in more danger with me here, now."

"Even if that's true, we're in this together," Styx said. "Now, come on. Time for your pills."

"Don't want more of that fuzzy-headed shit," he mumbled, tried to push Styx away. But suddenly, Law's hand was on his cock again and he moaned, the protests washing away.

Fuck, he was a sucker on pain pills. And horny, too. "What the hell are in those things?"

Law stroked faster. "Whatever it is, you think you'd want more, not less."

"Yeah."

"Take the pills," Styx said, and Paulo opened his mouth and complied, taking some water, then he lay back and let Law continue his long, slow strokes while Styx sucked his nipple into his mouth.

"Shit." He knew he needed to stay still in order to

minimize the pain and maximize the pleasure.

"You'll feel good soon…then you'll sleep," Law told him, and he practically purred under the men's touches.

He'd only been away for days, but it felt like a lifetime. And so he let them take him, coming more quickly than he wanted to and basking in the warmth of that.

When he woke again, it was still dark and the room was nearly so, save for the dimmed light on the night table. If not for that, he wouldn't have been able to see Law sleeping on the pillow next to him. Paulo reached out to run fingers through his hair, and he opened his eyes.

"Sorry. I'm sorry." It was all Paulo could think to say.

"Me too." Law propped on his elbow, traced a finger along Paulo's cheek. "You were out like a light."

"How long?"

"At least fourteen hours."

"Hate those pills."

"Yeah, well, you're pretty banged up." He paused. "Tomcat said to call him if you remember anything else."

He remembered everything he needed to—it was the escape that wasn't clear. But the intel—he held that close, because it could be the break they needed.

He didn't want any of this to be for nothing.

He closed his eyes for a second and when he opened them again, Law was holding out a cup with a straw.

"Drink. Or I'll put in an IV."

"Bossy." He drank the cup of ginger ale down and

realized he was actually hungry. "Any food?"

"Yeah." Law smiled, passed him his phone. "Styx is making dinner—you make your call."

He guessed Law wanted to listen in, doubted he'd leave even if Paulo asked, so he didn't.

"Dude, you got me in so much trouble with those two," Tomcat started as soon as he answered. "Tell me it was worth it."

"It was." Paulo rattled off the names and dates he'd heard the men muttering to one another in some sort of code that he'd sifted through in his mind over and over during the hours he'd been tied until he'd realized they'd been talking bank account numbers and dates. "I think these will help."

Law was staring at him, muttering, "How the hell did you get all that?" as Tomcat said, "Fucking brilliant," and hung up the phone.

Paulo hung up on his end, handed it back to Law. "We're close."

"Don't even think about it," Law warned. "You're sitting the next round out."

"I didn't come this far to back down," Paulo ground out, but the fact that he could barely move, thanks to what happened to be bruised ribs, made the show less impressive than he'd hoped.

"We almost lost you," Law told him. "Couldn't live with ourselves if that happened."

"Don't pull the guilt card."

"It's way more than guilt," Styx said from where he stood in the doorway. "Have you looked in a mirror lately?"

"There were four of them," Paulo confirmed. "So all things considered, I don't think I look too bad."

Law smirked at that, and Styx just shook his head. "I'm going to kill Tomcat for this."

"Why? We're a step closer to finding out where your father lives. You wouldn't let me do it by myself, and you and Law couldn't do it without being found out. I have no regrets—not one." Paulo spoke so fiercely, breathed in too hard and saw stars. Law held him carefully by the shoulders.

"Baby, we know why you did it, okay?"

"Don't patronize me." His teeth clenched and he was sweating from the exertion.

Styx put his lips on Paulo's shoulder, kissed gently. "I'm sorry this spilled over into your life."

Paulo rested his head against Styx's shoulder. "We're close to this being over—so close."

"I know. And Tomcat and I are planning... But I'm not doing anything until you're better," Styx told him.

Paulo nodded and didn't push anything further. "My family—"

"They're okay," Styx assured him. "They're in a safe house for now until this is all figured out."

"God, my father must hate that."

"Pretty much," Styx agreed. "But they're happy you're alive, Paulo. Your mom wants you to call her."

Paulo snorted and even that hurt, so he shut up and lay there and tried to absorb what had happened over the past few days. Except the last bits were all…fuzzy. "In the building…at the end…"

Styx stared at him. "You don't remember?"

"It's still hazy, but I remember shots."

"You got out of your bonds. You shot one guy and were taking on the other two when Tomcat came in to help and took out the fourth," Styx said. "You were a goddamned hero. You put a hell of a dent in my father's organization. He keeps things pretty close to the vest, doesn't like to hire a lot of outside help. It's taken him years to build up those men. He's vulnerable now."

"Good. So are you two going to treat me like I'm made of glass for much longer?"

"Yes," Law and Styx told him together.

"You can't put yourself out there like that—it could've easily ended badly. You set yourself up for this," Styx said.

"I had a plan," Paulo mumbled.

"What? Stopping fists with your body?" Styx was angry but concerned. Shook his head. "No more of this shit—I'm in charge of this op."

Both men stared at him. "Well, I am."

"Together. That's the only way," Law said firmly.

"Last time I looked, neither of you were CIA. They kind of frown on former military and cops trying to help." Paulo watched Law stare Styx down. "Ah, come on, Law."

"You promised me. And you don't go back on those. The Styx I knew never did."

Styx sighed, stared at the ceiling. "He still doesn't."

"Good." Law looked back at Paulo. "Don't worry about anything."

"Yeah, okay," he muttered. "Because that's worked so well for all of us."

When Paulo woke again, Styx was lying with him, reading a paperback biography of some rock star. Paulo had managed to turn so he was pressed against the man, but Styx didn't appear to have minded.

Instead, he put down his book and let Paulo shift to get even more comfortable. Handed him the soda from the side of the bed. And another pain pill—a half—which he took reluctantly since everything was throbbing again and not in a good way.

"Can't wait till I don't have to take these anymore," he muttered.

"Sleep's good for you—means you're healing," Styx told him, brushed the hair from Paulo's forehead gently.

"Don't be angry with Tomcat. I made the decision to help him."

"Yeah, I know." Styx shook his head. "My father ruins everything he touches. I don't want him anywhere near you or Law again."

"I know you don't think of him as a father...but even though you know his real name, you never use it. Why?" Paulo asked, and Styx smiled wryly.

"It's like the devil—you should never say his name out loud unless you want him to appear."

It was Paulo's turn to smile a little. "I know what you mean." It had been a long time since he'd mentioned his father's name. McMannus was a common last name, so that wasn't a big concern, but Big Pat, as he was nicknamed... well, Paulo rarely let himself think about the man.

The descriptions in the paper, at the trial, they'd been horrifying. "I couldn't talk to him after that day in court. The last words my father sneered to me were that I'd never escape his legacy—or the fact that I was queer." Paulo had no issue with the queer thing, but to be a part of that man's family... "He's right—I can't escape it. They think I've got that in me. Telling them I'm gay makes things worse in a whole different way."

"You can't spend your life making up for him. That's not on your shoulders," Styx said.

"I'd say ditto, but I'm betting you'll tell me your situation is very different."

Styx snorted at that but didn't look happy.

Paulo continued anyway. "Why didn't your father go after Damon?"

"He knew we weren't lovers. I would've died if he'd hurt

Damon, but he knew it wasn't the same thing. By that point, Damon was out of the house a lot, too. He was working different clubs—more the BDSM crowd while Law and I were working Greg's, which were your typical dance-and-fuck-in-the-back-room variety," Styx explained. "He had pictures. Of me and Law together. Made it look so damned dirty."

Paulo nodded, thought back to his own family's reaction to his admission. "My family hasn't talked to me since the day I came out. I think sometimes that what my father did to that prisoner...I feel like it was because of me. All the rage was supposed to be directed at me."

He hadn't realized his breath had come fast, and it had been the first time he'd ever admitted that. "There was so much hate in what he did. If he'd gotten his hands on me..."

"Don't go there," Styx said. Paulo hadn't even realized he'd moved to him. "Paulo, man, you're shaking like a leaf. Here."

Styx wrapped the blanket around both of them and just held him close.

"Why would he do that? I was the same kid—the same one he took hunting," Paulo heard himself saying, his voice thin, and he hadn't known the wounds had been this deep.

"It's nothing you did," Styx soothed. "It's his hang-up. You didn't deserve that treatment."

"I shouldn't...compared to what you and Law went through—"

"Hey—don't do that. I want you to let it out, baby. Get it all out and put it behind you." Styx rubbed his back and cradled him and he let it go, his face buried against Styx's chest. "I'm sorry your parents are so fucked up."

Paulo nodded and wished he could just stay like this, half suspended in sleep from the meds. "Fucking hate these pills. Like truth serum."

Styx chuckled. "This time, the truth will set you free."

Paulo raised his eyes. "Thanks. For listening. Jesus, when I first met you—first heard about you… Let's just say you're the last person I'd ever thought I'd be admitting shit like this to."

"But you are."

Paulo's next words came out in a rush. "Law loves you. I could never take you from him, couldn't let that happen. I would walk away first. I'm ready to. When it's time, you've got to help me make him let me go."

"To me."

"Yeah. If you leave him again, for any reason, I'll hunt your ass down. But you guys belong together."

"He's fallen for you," Styx told him quietly.

"He'd already fallen for you. It's one thing to compete with a ghost. Another with you, flesh and blood."

Paulo felt the blood seeping down his side, looked down. "Shit, I busted a stitch." He was busy grabbing for another piece of gauze and Styx helped him, pressing it tight to make sure the bleeding stopped.

"Lie back—you're doing too much."

"Talking?" Paulo asked, but he didn't fight when Styx pushed him to the pillows gently. The conversation—the confessions—had all worn him out and he let himself drift off, secure in the knowledge that Styx and Law would watch over him.

15

Styx watched Paulo sleep for a little while, and he must've fallen asleep himself, because when he woke, it was with a start.

Confused, he looked down at the man lying next to him, saw tattoos and blood and reached out tentatively to touch him…and this was all so familiar…and all too real.

"Styx, what is it?" Law asked.

Law? What the hell was he doing here?

Styx looked at him and then back at the man in bed… the tattoos, the blood…

"Styx, you're so pale, man—look like you're seeing a ghost."

But Styx didn't answer, reached out to touch the young man's face…jerked back and then slowly let his fingers settle along his temple. "He's still warm," he murmured. "I have to save him…thought he was dead."

"He's alive, Styx."

"I thought Kyle died."

"This is Paulo, not Kyle," Law said calmly, his voice

strong and soothing. Slowly, Styx came back to reality as he blinked, stared down at the younger man's temple. The gunshot wound was gone and in its place, unmarred skin.

The tattoos…the blood…

His body shuddered under the weight of the memory— it was tremendous, and he wasn't sure if he could bear the truth, let alone say it out loud.

Paulo stirred under Styx's touch, looked confused and no doubt felt the distress. But all he did was reach out to touch Styx's hand, and Law took the other in his.

"I remember something," Styx said hoarsely.

God, the memories were flooding back from that night, like watching a slow-motion video of the events.

"Right in front of me," he whispered. "Because I refused to get involved. He killed him."

Neither man pushed him, and he spent the next few moments trying to breathe through what felt like a straw.

"My father…that night…the blood on my shirt when I woke up was my…" His lover. His first. Kyle. "Kyle. He was older than me. Twenty. He was…I was in love with him. He was going to take me away."

"Your father killed him in front of you?" Law breathed out the question.

Styx nodded. "He killed him because of me."

Paulo struggled to sit up and winced, and Styx put his hand out to the man's shoulder. "Please, stay down. Bad enough seeing you hurt the first time."

"Then come down here—both of you."

"Bossy," Styx muttered, but both he and Law complied. This time, it was Styx in the middle with both men holding him, letting him tell the story at his own pace.

He lay there a long time before he spoke again. "It was the night I first met Greg…before I ended up on the bench in Central Park. I was home—in a room with a white rug and black leather furniture and I should recognize it as my house, but I still don't. And I was standing there, telling my father no and my father was telling me, 'You're dead to me.'"

"What wouldn't you do?"

"Work with him. For him. I was horrified when he told me what he expected of me—and why. I didn't understand the consequences of the refusal…never suspected he would…" Styx shook his head. "It happened so fast. He said, 'You have one chance to decide.' He dragged Kyle in front of me and Kyle—he looked so fierce, told my father to get the fuck off him. That he had no power over him, but I knew better. And I just said, 'You wouldn't…'"

You wouldn't.

He'd said it in a tone of horror, blurted it out in shock.

His father had smiled and then he'd just done it.

The blood, Kyle's face…the sound of the shot echoing in his ears. His father letting go of Kyle…his lover crumpling to the ground.

Styx moved forward, catching him halfway down,

cradled his head against his chest and stomach and cried.

"Pussy," his father spat. "Shouldn't have expected anything from a faggot. Both of you."

"I should've saved him."

"You weren't—you reacted—you didn't think he'd do it."

Styx was still staring at Paulo. "The blood."

"Styx, I'm okay—I'm fine," Paulo was telling him.

Styx buried his face into Paulo's shoulder. "It was the tattoos that reminded me. Kyle had a sleeve."

Law burrowed against his back. There were more memories there, waiting like soldiers to fall, but Styx was weary, too much to pull back the curtain.

"We'll get him, Styx," Paulo promised, his voice fiercer than Law or Styx had ever heard it. "I swear, I will not let him haunt you any longer—you've given up too much already."

Styx nodded, too tired to say anything more about it. "I have to talk to Tomcat—give him Kyle's name. The more ammo against him, the better. Besides, it might give some closure to Kyle's family."

The men didn't argue when he got off the bed and went to make the call.

If Law hadn't been sure about the three of them before this, Paulo's words to Styx sealed it for him. And despite the hell Styx was going through, they would work together and finish this.

"He goes nowhere alone." Law glanced out the bedroom door Styx had just exited.

"None of us goes anywhere alone," Paulo added softly. "The three of us need to stick together."

"Says the man who went rogue."

"Yeah, well." Paulo rubbed the back of his neck and winced. "Fucker's got to be taken down—he's the one running the show."

Law would cut off the man's head. "I'll do this for him, the way he did for me."

Paulo's eyes met his, the soft look of surprise more for the fact that Law knew it than anything.

"I never knew for sure until now," Law said. "Based on your reaction, I'm guessing I was right. He saved me from having to do the job and getting sucked back into that pit of hell."

"So what's the plan?"

"I'm the best bait there is."

Paulo didn't argue, just nodded. "We'll lure him, and then we'll make sure he can't hurt Styx again, ever, and then, back to reality."

"Because this isn't?"

"No."

"This is as real as it gets," Law argued. "If we can get through this, don't you think we can deal with anything?"

"I do," Paulo said.

"You're scared," Law told him. "I am too. But fuck, the three of us need to stop that. We can't let fear rule our lives or we'll miss out on the important shit, like each other."

"I can't believe what his father did. Actually, no, I think it's sadder that I believe it."

"Yeah, I know what you mean. Maybe this will be the start of him really letting the ghosts go."

"You can help him with that."

"So can you." Law stared at Paulo pointedly. The younger man still had bruises that were turning lighter shades of purple and blue and yellow, all signs of how close he'd come to losing him.

Signs of just how good at his job he was. He couldn't lose someone else to the goddamned CIA, but if that's what Paulo wanted…

What about what you want?

Yeah, it was time to do some convincing. "We were looking for you because we were worried. But it's more than that. We wanted you with us."

"You've got me, at least until I'm up and around on my own."

"You don't understand. When I say with us, I mean… well, beyond this clusterfuck."

"What—all three of us live…together? Be together?" Paulo paused. "You look so goddamned serious, but you've got to be fucking with me."

Law leaned over, began stroking a hand through his hair. "I'm not. I would never do that to you."

"Keep doing that."

"Touching you?"

"Yeah. Missed that. Like that you're not pushing me away the way you were in the beginning."

"I missed it too," Law whispered. "Don't run anymore."

"It's too crowded...too many people in your bed."

Law touched the bruise under Paulo's eye. "Normally I'd agree, but now I'd have to say with you and Styx, there's no such thing. I like that kind of crowded, Paulo. I want it."

"I've never committed either," Paulo said. "I didn't think I would ever be able to. I was always looking for a way to bolt."

"I won't keep you anywhere you don't want to be...but fuck, I want you to stay," Law implored.

Law hadn't been with Styx for ten years—making Paulo a part of it hadn't been in the plan—hell, there hadn't been one, but now that it was unfolding, he realized nothing had ever felt this right.

"Where can this go?" Paulo asked.

"Forward," Law said quietly. "We move forward together."

"All three of us?"

"It's been happening already," Law reminded him, and while that was truth Paulo would obviously concede to, the circumstances surrounding it had been extraordinary. Dangerous.

What would happen when things went back to normal?

"I don't think normal's anything the three of us need to worry about." Law smiled a little. "Are you willing to try?"

"What's my choice? To give up two men I…" He paused and then stared at Law. "To give up two men I love. I don't want to do that."

"I love you, Paulo. Now we just have to convince that stubborn one that he's better off with us than without."

"How is this supposed to work?" Paulo asked. "Are we supposed to share you—one night in my bed, one night in his?"

Law didn't know what to say, because to him, that didn't sound bad at all. These two men both tugged at him—hard—and he didn't know what direction to turn.

"You told me you were a switch," Paulo said. "Is that only for him?"

Law stared at Paulo with those intense blue eyes, a storm of emotion coming over them. "No."

"So you'd let me top you, then?"

Law hesitated. "It's not about not wanting you to fuck me. That's not what my switching's all about."

"It's about letting yourself be dominated…trusting someone enough to lose total control," Paulo said, and Law blinked. "What? You think I don't fantasize about that? You know I do—I told you in the diner one of the first times I met you that I wanted to tie you down so you couldn't get away."

Law swallowed hard. "I don't like to lose control."

"Yeah, no shit." Law moved away at Paulo's words but Paulo caught him. "S'okay, Law. It really is."

"If you want to fuck me, you could've just asked."

"I just want you—doesn't matter how. Christ, am I not allowed to ask questions?"

Law swallowed and Paulo saw the walls that had started to go up again fall a bit. "You can ask."

"I guess we all have to do a better job of letting our guards down," Paulo said.

"I've held back," Law admitted. "I was scared you'd find out who I really am. A scared, abused boy who's still fucked up, all these years later."

"You don't seem all that fucked up to me," Paulo told him. "You've made a good life for yourself."

"I've backed away from any chance of real love…"

"Until now," Paulo said.

"Yeah, until now," Law echoed. "Ironic that Styx came back into the picture right now."

"I don't think there's anything about coincidences that are coincidence."

"God, you sound just like Greg," Law muttered.

"Is that good?"

"Greg would've approved of Paulo…of all of this that's

happening between us." Styx's voice took them by surprise and they turned to find him watching both of them carefully.

"I thought you were on the phone," Law said.

"I made my call. But I don't like missing things. I've spent too long doing that—I won't let him take away anything more, including time with both of you."

"You really think this will work—the three of us?" Paulo asked.

"I think it already is," Styx said, and Law added, "How can it not? I won't let either of you go. I spent too long without anyone. Let's just call this fate's way of making up for lost time."

At Law's words, Styx came forward slowly, moving like the predator he was, stripping his shirt off and sinking into the mattress between Paulo's legs.

"Oh, fuck." Paulo reached down to thread his hands through Styx's hair, which was a shade darker than his but not as dark as Law's. Styx's hair color was right in between his and Law's…and that's not where Styx himself was any longer, not between them, but with them. And what a difference that made. "I don't know what you both want from me."

"You. That's all. It's that simple."

"I'm used to running."

"I'm used to pushing people away. But I think we can change," Law told him. "I never thought I'd find one love of my life, never mind two."

Styx slid Paulo's cock in his mouth and hummed with satisfaction.

Law was kissing him and Styx was sucking him, urging him on with his tongue and a slight scrape of teeth, and Paulo's cock throbbed in his mouth.

But instead of finishing the blowjob, Styx rose, told Law, "I want to watch Paulo fuck you," and no, the man didn't miss a trick, had no doubt been listening to them for longer than they'd thought.

Law shook his head, his cheeks flushed, and he looked ready to bolt. Paulo understood the strong reaction and he put his hand out on Law's shoulder to reassure him.

"I can't," Law whispered finally, his voice raw.

"You should do this," Styx said but Paulo jumped in quickly with, "He doesn't have to."

"No, he doesn't," Styx agreed. "But I think he wants to try it with you."

Both men looked at Law, whose expression was still dark. And even as Styx moved behind Law and started to strip him, he told Paulo, "You'll have to lead him. You'll have to be in charge."

Paulo watched Law's clothes come off, and the man sank against Styx's chest, closed his eyes as Styx's hand went to his cock and stroked a few times.

Paulo's throat went dry as Styx flipped Law and gave Paulo a wickedly hot look before he began tonguing the man's ass. Law bucked, maybe would've moved, but Styx held him fast by the hips as he worked.

"Jesus, Styx," Law breathed, and then he uttered a cross between a whimper and a moan as Styx continued to work him over. Law could come just from that, Paulo decided, wondered if it was Styx's plan. "Please, touch my dick."

But Styx wouldn't and Law couldn't lift an arm off the bed.

Paulo couldn't keep his hand off his own cock while he watched Law squirming and begging and Styx hadn't stopped his assault.

Law cried out when he came hard, his body practically vibrating, and God, the man looked so beautiful fighting and ultimately giving in to his lust.

Styx didn't waste time, had lubed his cock already, and he rose and drove into Law hard, while the man was still recovering from his orgasm. Law's head rose and he stared into Paulo's eyes as Styx took him.

"Put your cock in his mouth, Paulo," Styx directed, told him again when he hesitated.

Paulo approached, knelt on the bed—no small feat the way it was rocking—and Law licked his bottom lip as Paulo's cock bobbed in front of his face. He guided it into Law's mouth and Styx slowed his movements, allowing

Law to deep throat him, hum around his cock with Styx's languid movements. Paulo gripped Law's hair, more turned on by the fact that Law was trapped between them…that Law allowed it, felt safe enough with both of them to let go like this.

"Come in his mouth," Styx told him. "Then you're going to take his ass."

At his words, Law groaned around Paulo's cock and Paulo came, hard enough to see stars, calling out Law's name.

Law had forgotten how quickly Paulo's cock rebounded—the man always seemed to stay hard even after several orgasms, and he knew Styx was right, that he needed to let this happen, needed to let Paulo take him.

He sat up, still on his knees, as Styx went to the bathroom. He heard water running as Paulo massaged his back and when Styx came back after cleaning himself, Paulo and Styx switched places. As Styx lay down in front of him, Law felt Paulo's hands on his shoulders, pressing him down toward Styx's cock.

Being used by these men was more than a fantasy and it didn't take much for Law to take Styx's cock in his mouth. Paulo's hands remained on his back, half massage, half to keep him in place. And when Paulo's fingers skimmed the seam of his ass, Law jumped a little, but the hand held him firm.

He hummed around Styx's cock, felt the man jump and he smiled because he liked throwing Styx off his game. Especially when Law was so thrown himself.

Paulo's lubed fingers circled his hole—Law wanted to close his legs, but Paulo's thighs held his far apart and in order to keep his balance he needed to keep his palms flat.

Styx's hands were in his hair, and then he heard it, glanced up and saw Styx and Paulo kissing above him. God, they were hot together, different shades of blond.

Paulo's finger was quickly followed by a second and then Paulo was pulling him up by his hair so he was in a tall kneeling position, Paulo's mouth hot on his neck, hands manipulating him open, and he heard himself moaning.

Styx was tugging his own cock, watching the men, and Law remembered what was happening, and he struggled to move. Paulo didn't hold him fast, his fingers slipped from his ass but Styx stopped Law from moving away completely.

"Let him, Law," Styx said quietly. "You have to."

For this to work, he did. There could be no boundaries between them, not like this. Law had to be able to switch.

Law stared at Paulo. "Do you want this?"

"You know I do," Paulo told him. "You know you do, too. Can you let it happen? Because this is a fantasy I've had since I saw you. Tying you down…making you helpless to stop me from fucking you."

"Tie him down," Styx told him and Law swallowed hard, but he didn't protest. Not out loud, anyway, but his muscles tensed and his eyes flashed with a slight panic that Styx quickly smoothed over with a kiss and a murmur in his ear.

Law moved to the head of the bed, put his hands up to grab the headboard and Paulo accepted the handcuffs from Styx.

"It won't hold him otherwise," Styx said, and Law nodded.

"Do it, Paulo. Quickly."

Paulo didn't hesitate. Cuffed Law's wrists and had the chain snake through an opening on the headboard. And then sat back, admiring the man all stretched out and waiting. "You ready?"

Law gave a small smile. "No."

But he spread his legs anyway, as Styx stayed close, smoothed his hair from his forehead as Paulo mounted him. The younger man leaned in and kissed Law, so sweet and still hard enough to show Law that he meant business. He wasn't letting up until he'd gotten all the way in—literally and figuratively—and Law finally gave up the ghost and let it happen.

Law was already sore, and even though Paulo went slowly, he still froze up for a few seconds.

"Breathe, baby," Paulo whispered, and Law nodded and swallowed and closed his eyes. Willed himself to relax and felt Paulo push fully inside of him. But the younger man waited for Law to move before he did. Bucked his hips up to see how it would feel, and Paulo groaned his name.

It felt damned fine. Paulo began to rock against him and the resistance fell from his body as Paulo's cock bumped his prostate a few times with a calculated move meant to take the breath from Law's body.

Success, and in those seconds, Law forgot everything—that he was supposed to not want this, that he needed all the control, and he let Paulo take him. Styx undid the cuffs at some point and Law put his hands on Paulo's shoulders. His legs wrapped around the younger man's waist, and he was vaguely aware that he was telling Paulo to go faster. And then someone called him bossy and it became a tangle of arms and legs before Law could say anything more. Styx moved behind Law, leaning in to stroke Law's cock as his own erection rubbed Law's back, while Paulo continued fucking him.

Law came hard, felt himself spurt on his stomach—it hit his chin and someone licked it off and then he was turned and put on his hands and knees again, and Paulo was back inside him, riding him, and by the end he'd collapsed on his elbows, ass in the air.

And after Paulo came, Styx entered him. Law could feel the difference with the piercing and he moaned and accepted the fucking as Paulo moved behind him, and God, it was Paulo's cock against his back and Styx inside of him and he was between the men he loved.

16

The plan had been to let Styx's father get comfortable again—Tomcat hadn't wanted him suspicious, and so the three men remained at the cabin together for several more days as Paulo healed and their bond grew tighter.

Now, with Styx on the phone with Tomcat and their supervisor in the living room, Law finished a sandwich and Paulo sat across from him, drumming his fingers on the table.

"He'll tell us everything," Law said.

"I know. I just hate waiting."

Law nodded. "You still planning on going private after this?"

"Yeah. I don't want to do bail bonding. PI seems the best route, and I can take the cases I want."

"I could work with you," Law said.

"You, a PI?"

"I was in the Army, you asshole."

Paulo laughed. "I know—I just like hearing you say that. You said that on one of the nights I cornered you outside the club. You know, when you were playing one-man Army."

"I wasn't playing."

"You're serious? About the business?"

"Yeah, I am. I'm betting Damon would be too. We definitely don't want to do the club thing again." And Damon doing this could help ease the times when Tanner was away.

"What about Styx?" Paulo asked. "Do you think…?"

"Do I think he'll stay in the CIA? Maybe. I can't ask him to leave."

Paulo nodded, obviously agreed, but it was definitely something to consider and worry about. Styx would be gone for long periods of time without either man knowing where he was or when he was coming back—Styx's position in the CIA was like Delta Force on steroids.

He heard Styx wrapping things up on the phone, and told Paulo, "I need your help. I've got an idea for back-up for me and Styx, and I need you to distract him for a while so I can call Damon."

"And you're not telling Styx? Because remember, that didn't end all that well for me last time," Paulo said, and Law nodded.

"I know, but I'm doing it anyway. Styx would never want it like this, but we're going to need all the help we can get." Law looked at Paulo. "Think you're well enough to keep him busy?"

"I think I'm up for the job."

"A real hardship." Law smirked as Styx ended his call and began to work on stoking the fire. Paulo waited until Styx finished and sat back on the couch. The throwaway phone was on the counter, and Paulo watched Law pocket it and then go into the bedroom on the other side of the cabin—the spare room they rarely used—and he heard the TV go on.

Paulo wandered into the living room and stared out the window.

"Hey, you all right?" Styx asked and Paulo shrugged.

Styx was by his side immediately, looking so concerned Paulo felt guilty.

"Pain?" he asked.

"A little."

Styx's arms went around him. "Where's Law?"

"He's watching a movie. Figured he needed a little space."

"He's always liked his alone time—don't take it personally," Styx told him.

"I don't. I mean, I haven't known him that long but—"

"You know him well enough. That's what intrigued him about you from the start."

Paulo turned to look at him. "That simple?"

Styx shrugged. "Not many people took the time to find out about him...they always wanted to fuck him, to get fucked by him. But they never took the time to know him. And although he always protests he doesn't want that, he really does."

That made Paulo smile. "I've never done that for anyone. Never wanted that."

"There's something about him."

"There's something about you too." Paulo reached up and touched a small scar above Styx's eyebrow.

Styx leaned in and kissed him, long, slow hot kisses that made Paulo immediately forget the reason he'd actually started this and made him fall into the natural rhythm being around this man always put him in.

Styx pulled Paulo's sweats down easily and then worked on his own jeans, stepped out of them and urged Paulo toward the bedroom.

If that bed could talk…holy shit.

Styx sat against the headboard, and as Paulo watched, he lubed his condomed cock and then motioned to Paulo to come closer.

Paulo straddled the man and Styx fingered his ass. They hadn't been inside him since before he'd left them…but Paulo was more than ready.

He let Styx drive him in and out of his mouth—it was alternating fingers to prostate, tongue inserted into his piss hole until he was ready to climb out of his skin it felt so good.

Styx was smiling around his cock and Paulo hadn't realized how loud his moans were until then, and his cheeks heated, but he didn't stop. Couldn't.

"That's it, baby, climb on," Styx urged, and Paulo did,

taking Styx inside of him, inch by inch, reveling in the slow burn, his fingers digging into Styx's shoulders.

When he'd taken Styx's cock to the hilt, Paulo stayed still for a long moment, adjusting to the girth. Styx played with his nipples, sucked on one while teasing the other between his thumb and forefinger.

Paulo buried his face in Styx's hair and began to move up and down, enjoying the delicious friction—part pain but mostly pleasure. Styx's hands moved to Paulo's hips to rock him faster and faster until Paulo spurted, coating both their stomachs…and moments later, Styx let go, holding Paulo tightly as his orgasm pulsed into the condom, still deep inside Paulo.

They remained like that for a long time, Paulo unwilling to move and Styx simply holding him.

"Thanks," Paulo whispered finally. It was the first time he'd been fully alone with Styx before, during and after a sexual encounter…and he guessed they'd needed this. It was easy to be compatible in a threesome—and Paulo had known there were sparks between them, but now he knew there was more, for sure.

"Not done." Styx stood with Paulo still in his arms and Paulo didn't protest when Styx walked him to the bathroom, sat him on the edge of the tub and let the water run.

It was a large, Jacuzzi-like tub, and Paulo climbed in at Styx's urging, and Styx joined him, the two men sitting opposite each other, legs twined together, the water bubbling up around them like a warm embrace.

"Feeling better?" he asked, and Paulo nodded.

"I get tense when you plan with Tomcat," he admitted, and Styx could appreciate both the sentiment and his honesty.

"Tomcat's really impressed with you," Styx told him. "I am, too. In all different kinds of ways."

"Now that I've cleared your background check, right?"

"You haven't forgiven me for that yet?"

"I can understand why you felt the need." Paulo stared into the dark green eyes. "Law would've found out eventually."

"Tomcat said you want to open a PI business."

Paulo nodded. "I figured I could do some good. I didn't want to deal with bail bonds shit, but I could do some side work for the department this way. Keep my hand in it."

"The CIA's been asking questions."

Paulo raised his eyebrows. "About me? As in, recruitment?"

"Yes." Styx's gaze was steady. "As much as I don't want you in this game, it wouldn't be fair not to let you know. Your past wouldn't matter in there. It's only about you and what you can do for the agency."

"It was never like that on the force. It was all about your

past—who you were. What you were." He shook his head. "It's a whole different world."

"Sounds like it."

"I spent too much time trying to fit in instead of just finding someplace…people who accepted me. I don't think that's too much to ask."

"No, it's not." Styx rubbed his calf with his foot. "Were you ever close with your father?"

"I used to try—especially when we'd go hunting together," he said. "That was a big thing in my family—the fact that my father finally had a son to hunt with after three daughters."

"Did you like it?"

"I did. Mainly because I thought…I thought maybe he'd be so close to me that when I came out, it wouldn't matter." He paused. "He used to talk about it all the time—fags. But his bigotry really knew no bounds—race, creed, religion… unless you were exactly like him and his cop buddies, you were out."

"Took a lot of courage to come out with him like that."

"I figured the longer I took to make the break, the more it would hurt. There was no way I could've lived a lie forever. I'd rather be alone." And that's what he'd been for a long time.

"Even your sisters wouldn't speak to you?"

He shook his head. "Nah. They were my father's babies, you know? Did what he said, thought what he thought.

I mean, hell, I guess life is pretty easy when it works out that way. I'm just glad those teenage years are dead and buried, because those memories…" He trailed off and Styx understood.

"My first memory was waking up on a park bench. Less than twenty-four hours later, I'd fallen in love and I never stopped."

Paulo smiled. "Law's special—it's easy to recognize."

"And you were going to give him up for me."

"If it made him happy."

"What about your happiness?"

"That's never mattered much."

"It matters to Law," Styx said. "Matters to me, too."

"Why didn't you ever ask your father about your past?"

"Don't want to know," Styx said. "It was bad enough that I know what I know. If he'd never found me…if he'd just let me go…"

Then he would've been with Law, still. Maybe, or maybe the Army and the CIA would've still been a part of their lives, tearing them apart anyway. He usually avoided the what-ifs, the regrets, because it was an unchangeable force and why waste energy?

But sometimes, in the dead of night, when he was all alone, he let it creep in and nearly strangle him.

"Don't go there," Paulo told him now and shit, he usually had a much better poker face. But the younger man was rising, water rippling off his still bruised and battered body.

He wrapped the towel around his waist and moved to sit on the tub ledge behind Styx in order to massage his shoulders.

"I'm supposed to be making you feel better."

"Who said?" Paulo dug his fingers into the muscles in his shoulders until Styx was practically purring. "I didn't mean to bring up memories. It's just…sometimes I wish I had none."

"I'm sure there are a lot of people who wish they could wipe out some memories." Styx ran his hands through his damp hair while watching Paulo balance on the edge of the tub. "The thing is, I could've done anything during that time. What if I took after my father? What if I killed people and I don't remember? It's a big, scary black hole and I don't know if I'm ever going to get it back."

"What do the doctors say?"

"They tell me that the mind's a funny thing. That my memories could show up at any given second, or they might never come back at all."

"So basically, they have no clue."

Styx snorted, leaned back and closed his eyes, the warm jets massaging his body. He was hard, which seemed to be a perpetual state while he remained around these two men.

His hand moved to Paulo's thigh as Paulo's hand went to the back of Styx's neck, giving a slow massage to the knots of tension he couldn't seem to get rid of.

"Nice," Styx murmured.

"Lean up a little," Paulo urged, and Styx did so, let Paulo

move behind him to put his feet in the water on either side and begin massaging Styx's slick back with capable hands. "You know what, Styx? You're nothing like your father—no memory of yours could ever make me believe that."

"You're that sure?" Styx wanted to believe the younger man so badly he ached.

"I'm as sure of that as you are that I'm nothing like mine."

That was a fact. Paulo's father was a sick bigot and Styx had run into a lot of men like that in his time. Paulo was hard-edged, a damned good detective according to both his records and his actions when Law and Styx were in danger. "Thanks, Paulo."

He looked up then, saw Law watching them both from the doorway, a small smile on his face.

"That's a nice picture." His voice was husky, his chest and feet bare, his jeans unbuttoned and his cock hard, as outlined by the soft, worn denim.

Paulo didn't stop his massage, which had turned into more of a caress along his shoulders and Styx leaned back against him, his head against Paulo's thigh so he could jerk himself.

He heard Paulo's breath quicken and Law's mouth opened a little. He unzipped his jeans and pushed so they fell to the ground, stepped out of them and into the tub with Styx. Pushed his hand away from his cock.

"Open me up," Law murmured. Paulo shifted, came back with lube for Styx's fingers and he played with Law's ass as

Law straddled him, the water making the lube dissipate a little.

Law groaned, leaned over Styx's shoulder to kiss Paulo, and then Paulo nipped Styx's ear while Law moved to kiss him.

"Yeah, that's it—fuck me with your hand," Law urged, moved up and down as Styx slid a third finger inside and just watched Law enjoying himself. Paulo's erection pressed to his upper back, and they'd take care of that in a bit. Right now, he needed to be inside Law, maneuvered the man so Law began to take Styx inside.

The men thrashed together, Law holding him tight and fucking himself on Styx's cock, and all Styx could do was let Law have his way. He stroked Law's cock between them and his own balls tightened and he came seconds after Law's orgasm, and Law pulled back, his breath coming fast, and he smiled.

Water had sloshed all over the floor. Paulo threw down towels as the men got out of the tub and then Styx carried him gently and walked with him to the bedroom. Law was right behind him and both men pressed their wet bodies tenderly along Paulo's, making him slippery—and happy—between them.

17

After the men cleaned up, Styx cooked them dinner and they sat around the table, eating pasta with the football game on mute in the background. They were all half dressed and each kept a gun close and the whole scene was so incongruous that Styx would've laughed if their situation hadn't been so serious.

He would have to leave them soon—his chest ached at the thought of it. He dropped his fork and pushed away to look out the window. The men had stilled behind him.

"It's too dangerous for you," Paulo said, and yeah, he should've known they were on to him.

"I can't think of any other way," Styx replied.

"Me," Paulo shot back. "Let me."

Both Law and Styx said no at the same time, and it was Law's turn to rise from the table.

"It's my turn. Tomcat agrees."

"Tomcat agrees?" Styx asked, and fuck, he would kill his partner.

"Yes. We have a plan," Law said, and even Paulo was

looking at Law strangely.

"When the hell did you talk to him?" Paulo demanded and then shook his head as Law motioned toward the bathroom.

"Suddenly, you can do what the CIA couldn't for all these years?" Styx pointed out. "Are you some sort of miracle worker?"

"Yeah, I think I am." Law looked between Paulo and Styx.

Neither man could deny what Law had done for them. But Styx tugged on Law's arm. "If something happened to you…"

"If something happened to either of you, I'd never fucking forgive myself," Law countered. "Look, Tomcat has my back. Your father already has me in his sights. He won't expect that I'll be fighting back. But I have to this time. And you both have to let me."

"When?" Paulo asked quietly.

"Another week. Tomcat's got intel that Styx's father will be back in the country by then. He's letting everything die down and he's been doing some recruiting," Law said, and Styx nodded.

"Only he doesn't realize that two of the men he's hired are CIA agents. Of course, he's refused to meet with them in person—this is all done through an intermediary. He's too damned smart and suspicious."

Paulo looked between the men. "I want to know the

entire plan. If I can't go in with you, I still want to be there—
to be close."

Neither man argued, and Styx sat next to him, and Law
began to talk through the specifics. As the plan began to
unfold, Styx actually started to believe there could be a
light at the end of the tunnel.

And afterwards? Would he be able to stay with the two
men? Would they want him?

"Suppose I never get my memory back?" he asked
suddenly, interrupting Law.

"Suppose you don't?" Law asked. "What would it
change?"

"Nothing," Paulo said quietly, with Law nodding in
agreement.

"You're not your father, Styx. I don't care what biology
says. You're no more like him than I'm like mine," Law told
him, and with that, Styx let Law finish detailing out their
next moves.

The week passed faster than Paulo wanted it to. He'd
been clinging to every goddamned second rather than
focus on the worry he felt for the two men, both of whom
would be part of the plan.

He still wasn't strong enough to help, and he was able to
admit that he'd be more of a hindrance than an asset. But

none of it sat well with him, and both Law and Styx knew it.

"Tomorrow," Styx had confirmed earlier when Paulo caught him packing. Paulo had nodded, turned away and caught sight of himself in the mirror. His eyes were shaded with circles from lack of sleep, and although his pain had lessened considerably, none of them had been sleeping well.

Tomcat had been putting out a trail of breadcrumbs for Styx's father and the men who worked for him... By tomorrow, the plan would be fully operational.

They would catch him this time. There was no other option.

Both Law and Styx had been working out with the weight bench—had been running on the treadmill to keep limber. But now, Paulo found them sitting on the couch, watching porn.

"Like we don't have enough real-life examples?" Paulo grumbled but he didn't turn away. Couldn't. Not when the younger boy on the screen was being fucked by two men. He sat forward to watched, aware that his own cock throbbed as the man went limp and the two men who surrounded him looked like they were in heaven.

He was well aware that he'd held his breath through the entire scene. If the two men weren't here with him, he'd no doubt rewind that section and jerk off to it...and he was thinking of doing so even with them here.

From the looks of the two men on the couch, he didn't

think they'd mind. "That was hot."

Law settled his gaze on him. "You were there the night it happened at the club."

Paulo nodded. It had been intense, a special presentation set up by two Doms and the sub they shared. They'd been so gentle to him—and rough at the same time, and Paulo remembered thinking he was going to come in his pants. "I didn't see you there," he said to Law.

"I was in the back, watching on camera." Law cleared his throat and smiled, and Styx laughed as he tugged Paulo closer. His hand ran over the bulge in his jeans as he stared up into Paulo's face.

"What do you think?" he asked, and Paulo's entire body overheated at those words.

"You guys are really thinking…both? With me?"

Law nodded, and holy shit, this could happen. Every time they pushed him past another self-imposed boundary, he thought he'd hit his last one. But this…what they were suggesting…

Shit. He sat on the edge of the couch, feeling the same lightheadedness he had when they'd first mentioned spanking to him. That was nothing compared to double penetration and still, his cock was hard. The flesh was more than willing.

"You don't have to, baby," Styx told him and Law echoed the sentiment.

The men were leaving him behind tomorrow—not

literally, of course. Paulo would be as close to the mission as he could be, guarded by CIA agents. But it wouldn't be the same.

They had tonight, and after this, who knew if this spell—this bond—would somehow collapse under the weight of the real world.

"I want to," he heard himself say. He stood, stripped his shirt, and started unbuttoning and unzipping his jeans as he walked to the bedroom. He shook them off once he got close to the bed. The men had followed him inside, both of them stripping as well, and the room was warm… The heated need so palpable Paulo felt like he could swim through its thickness.

He forced himself to breathe. These men would take care of him. He was sure of it.

"If you need us to stop, use the word *red*, okay?" Law told him and Paulo nodded. Because yes, sometimes stop didn't mean stop during BDSM play—he'd told Styx to stop spanking him even though what he'd really wanted was to be smacked harder and longer.

A long, labored breath escaped him when Styx touched his ass, spread his cheeks and inserted a lubed finger inside, penetrating him with two then three after several minutes.

He tried to imagine what it would feel like to have both men inside him, stretching him to beyond the point of being filled. It would hurt…but from everything he'd seen firsthand, the bottom enjoyed himself.

"You sure you want this?" Law asked.

Both continued to push him past any limits he thought he had, and it only made him want more—from them and from himself. "Yeah. I want it."

Styx responded by sliding a fourth finger inside of Paulo, twisting his hand and making Paulo gasp and squirm against Law, Paulo's hands on the man's shoulders. "Gonna look so hot with both of us fucking you," Law told him.

He came on the spot, shot on his stomach and his chin, heard Styx murmur, "Holy fuck," from behind him. Law kissed him, and Paulo was still hard. He wasn't sure he'd ever been this turned on his life.

Styx moved away from him while he clung to Law, who kissed his neck, rubbed his back. And when Styx returned, he had a high chair with a back from the kitchen that he put against the wall. He held Paulo upright while Law got comfortable in the chair, sitting with his legs spread, cock jutting, and then Styx helped position Paulo so he was straddling Law face-to-face.

For a long moment, Paulo paused, and then he slid down on Law's cock, realized how locked in he'd be in this position, with Styx holding him down as he stood behind him.

He waited then, and both men simply remained still as if sensing the sudden panic and waiting until he worked through it. His ass adjusted to Law's girth slowly as Styx rubbed his shoulders and Law played with his nipples. His cock dripped precome and his chest was still sticky from coming, but then he heard himself say, "Go ahead," in a voice that didn't sound like his.

He hadn't expected Law's hips to buck up but the motion made him groan and curse at the same time and he forgot his fear for that moment, rocked against him and they were fucking, hard and fast, moaning.

And then Styx's finger slid inside him along Law's cock, and both Paulo and Law stiffened and groaned at the tightening sensation. When Law started rocking his hips up again, Styx added a second finger and the pressure—and the pleasure—was becoming more intense.

When he added the third, Paulo stopped moving, heard his breath harshen.

"S'okay, baby...you're doing great. You should see how fucking hot you look," Law told him.

"Maybe we should tape this," Styx added and even though Paulo knew they wouldn't, the thought that it could happen was enough to make another moan escape. "Ah, he likes that, the thought of us showing him off."

"We could put him on display—find a club around here who wants to put on a live show," Law added and Paulo shook his head no. "Baby, you've got no say right now."

Law's words shot through him like an orgasm, just as Styx's fingers left him and the head of his cock touched his hole.

Paulo sagged against Law. "Can't."

"You can do it, baby." Law stroked Paulo's hair. He was covered in a fine sweat from nerves from the enormity of what he was allowing them to do to him, and he felt like he'd come again the second Styx began to penetrate.

"Hold it together," Styx told him softly, because he knew. He was so close to Paulo, rubbing his shoulders with one hand, the other was fingering his ass around Law's cock, widening the hole for easier access.

When Styx pushed the head of his cock inside, all three men stilled and the only sound in the room was the harsh breathing, mainly from Paulo. He clutched at Law's shoulders, and before he could struggle away and hurt himself, Styx tightened his grip and pushed in farther with a long, slow slide.

"Halfway."

"God…please…" Paulo breathed, and it was more likely *God no*, but he wasn't saying that, seemed nearly incoherent and soon that would be with all pleasure. But Styx wasn't stopping, didn't until he was balls-deep inside Paulo, his cock rubbing Law's, and holy motherfucker, Paulo heard the keening groan escape his throat.

Law was breathing fast, his eyes wide, his hands on Paulo, caressing him. And then Styx began to pump his hips gently, rocking Paulo, and Law didn't move—couldn't—was as trapped as Paulo was by the sensations and the tightness and the fact that his cock was rubbing against Styx's.

When Paulo came, it was hard—almost painful—but the

most vibrant orgasm he'd ever had. He saw spots in front of his eyes, closed them as the contractions milked his dick, spilling his come on his stomach and Law's. He was aware the two men were both moaning as his contractions were tightening around both their cocks.

He felt the men come through the condoms. Law started first and Styx soon after, and it was almost like bareback, the sensations were so close to the surface. It was like he was drowning, his head down on Law's shoulders, his body boneless.

Styx pulled out slowly and Law remained inside of him to allow his ass to adjust. It would hurt too much if he didn't, and neither Law nor Paulo looked like they were in any shape to move.

Styx went to the bathroom, cleaned himself off and came back with a few wet washcloths and dry towels and then grabbed the sodas he'd left by the bedside.

First, he wiped Paulo down with the warm cloth and wrapped the towel around his back when he started to shiver.

"Drink this," he urged, and while Paulo moved from where he'd been draped across Law to do so, Styx wiped the come from their stomachs and dried them. Encouraged Law to drink soda as well, couldn't resist leaning in for an open-mouthed kiss with him, tasting the sugary Coke.

"Nice," Law murmured, and Styx had to agree.

"I'm going to help you off," Styx told Paulo. "Think

you're ready?"

Paulo nodded gamely even though he was nowhere near ready, and he let Styx practically carry him to the bed, his ass aching, his legs trembling and his mind trying to absorb the enormity of what he'd done. Styx curled up next to him while Law went to the bathroom, whispered, "Fucking fantastic," in his ear.

Paulo swallowed down tears, wondering where all the emotion was coming from—he hadn't shown this much when his father had disowned him, hadn't allowed anyone or anything over the past years since then to get to him like this.

"It's okay, you know—what you're feeling is normal," Styx told him.

"Now you read minds too," he muttered.

"You're not that hard to read." Styx paused and watched Law come back from the bathroom to stand next to him. "Not when it's the right people reading you."

"Love you both," he heard himself murmur, and wanted to take it back because maybe that was stupid.

"Love you both," Law echoed in his ear, followed by Styx's rendition, and it was that goddamned simple.

18

Law knew Styx wanted in on this, but both Law and Tomcat refused to let him.

"You're the one he wants most. He'd use Law to lure you in," Tomcat told him.

"And suppose he catches Law?" Styx argued.

"He won't, Styx. I told you, I can fight dirty." Law knew Styx wasn't underestimating him on purpose, but that nerves were getting the best of him now that they were so close to the end.

"Let me go in with you," Styx told Law.

"I don't want you near him. You said yourself, there's nothing he could tell you that you'd want to know. So don't go there. Let me do something for you, the way you've been protecting me all these years."

"You're not angry about that anymore?"

Law shifted. "I had your number. I could've asked you for more. I let my pride get in the way of all of this too. I have to bear some of the blame."

Styx hugged him, whispered, "I love you," into his ear

and Law said it back, out loud, and for a long while they remained like that.

"Worth the wait," Law said when they finally broke apart. Tomcat handed Law the gun, which he tucked into his pants. He was already wired and now, dressed in all black BDUs, he was more than ready.

"This started with me too—he made it about me. Now, it's going to finish with me."

There was nothing Styx could say to counter that. Law was too determined. He'd been trained to assassinate—he could protect himself at least as well as Styx, if not better. Still, he knew that for Styx, just the thought of Law putting himself in this much danger was almost too much for him to handle. He could see the worry written all over his lover's face, and although he didn't want to be the one to put it there, he knew he'd ultimately be the one to help take the worry away. For good.

"I'm going to be fine," Law told him firmly, put a hand on the back of Styx's neck and touched his forehead to Styx's, heard Styx's hitch of breath and gave the man a long moment to pull his shit together in front of his colleagues. Which Styx did, of course, by the time Law pulled away. "We all are."

"Going to command that to happen, are we?"

Law gave a wry smile. "Yes." With that, he left the van, which was parked several blocks from Styx's father's brownstone, and went through back alleys to reach the side door he'd planned on entering through. He could hear Tomcat and Styx in his ear, keeping contact as he worked in the dark.

He'd broken into more places than he cared to—or had been allowed to—admit. This one meant more than all the others put together. He held many lives in the hands that worked the double lock.

He spent twenty minutes bypassing the alarm system and getting inside while leaving it armed and in place, a personal favorite skill of his.

He needed to be inside with the alarm still set by the time Styx's father came home. And then he'd get the surprise of his life. "I'm in," he told the men, and then he moved around carefully, positioning himself in the hallway, with a wall to his back.

"He's on his way in," Styx said. "Law, please…"

Law switched off the mic, knowing it would do no good to hear Styx's voice. He needed to be on his game. And so he pushed Styx and Paulo from his mind, and he concentrated on the man in front of him, who walked directly toward him, pointing his gun at Law's chest.

Styx had been wrong about looking just like his father. The resemblance was there, for sure, but Styx's eyes were so much kinder.

As far as Law was concerned, blood wasn't that goddamned thick.

He resisted the urge to lunge forward and grab the man

around the neck, gun be damned. The hatred rose inside him for everything Styx's father had taken—no, had tried to take—from them. Styx's father hadn't succeeded up until this point, even though he'd managed to separate the men for far too long, and Law had to remember that. Because if he got too angry now to do his job, Styx's father would win.

"You're my son's little bitch." Styx's father sneered at him. "Should have taken you out when I had the opportunity. And I had so many of them. I would've killed that fag who you lived with too, if he hadn't died before I got the chance."

No one spoke about Greg like that... Law fisted his hands and Styx's father noticed. Laughed. "You know you're not supposed to show emotion. You were doing well for a while, but nothing like my son. He was the best."

"He is the best, no thanks to you."

"Yes, I'm the big bad wolf who corrupted that boy. If he'd stayed with me, he would've had the world. What does he have with you, besides a sin?"

Law laughed at that—the fact that this man considered their relationship a sin...and the killing was merely a job. "You're a sick son of a bitch. And really—you should've killed me when you had the chance. Because you're not going to get the chance now."

Law held his breath as Styx's father smiled—a chilling thing, because the man's eyes were as dead and colorless as coal. The gun rose a bit, centering between Law's eyes, and he would hold firm and trust.

Greg was watching over him. He had to believe that.

Styx's father finally spoke again. "You're a little too sure of yourself, son. You didn't think I knew you were here? You're not as sly as you think—you're on camera."

"But I'm not."

Styx's father froze as the gun came out of nowhere and touched the side of his head. He opened his mouth to speak but the shot stopped any words. There was blood spatter and brains on the wall, and Tanner let the man's body drop as he lowered the gun.

Tanner, who'd snuck in the back way before Law, after Law disabled the cameras. Once he was sure Tanner was safely inside, Law had allowed the cameras to capture him entering.

All part of the plan. And it had gone well but still, Law felt himself tremble at how close they'd all come.

"You okay?" Tanner asked.

"I think so."

"Then breathe, all right?" Tanner took his arm. "It's over, okay?"

"You risked too much," Law said.

"We all did. We always do. It's the way we live," Tanner said quietly. "Come on—the CIA can clean this shit up."

"Do you think…" Law paused. "I think he wanted to die."

"No matter what he wanted, he deserved to." Tanner guided Law out of the building as CIA agents moved past.

Tomcat clapped a hand on his shoulder, a grim look on his face.

Although this death was necessary, it always came at a high price.

Law turned back to Tanner. "I wanted to do it, but…"

"You've all had to deal with too much because of him. I'm the best choice. It's done." Tanner had always been a warrior, but he was different now. Stronger, more confident. Part Delta, part because of Damon's love and yes, they were all moving forward.

"I'm glad you called me," Tanner told him. "I owed you, for all your help with me and Damon. Granted, I never thought this would be the kind of debt you called in. But when you told me this was for Styx…well, Damon told me about you and him."

"Does Damon know you're here?" Either way, Damon was probably pissed Law didn't call him himself.

"He's outside. Backing me up. And he's not pissed—he's just worried." Tanner led him down the alley, where they met Damon.

"Sorry you had to cut your trip short," Law told him.

"This was more than worth it." Damon stepped forward and hugged Law. "I'll yell at you and Tanner later. Right now I'm just so goddamned grateful you're both okay."

"So am I." Styx's voice came up from behind Damon.

Law and Damon pulled apart and Damon whirled to face Styx. For a long moment, the men stared at each other, and then Damon said, "Good to see you, man. Really good."

They shook hands and then hugged. From behind Law, Tanner waited patiently, keeping an eye on all of them. Not so patiently, Styx came up next to Law, introduced himself to Tanner.

"Thank you," he said, and Tanner just nodded.

Styx turned back to Damon. "Damon. I owe you and Tanner. I'm—"

"Don't, Styx. Law told me everything. And now it's over, so don't let this time go to waste. I learned that lesson and it was almost too late." Damon glanced at Tanner and both men's faces practically glowed. "And then I learned that it's really never too late."

"I'm finding that out myself," Styx said. "Still, it would've been nice if Law and Tanner let me in on this before I had to watch it play out on video."

"We needed someone outside the situation, someone who didn't live through it, who could keep a cool head," Law explained. "Tomcat agreed. I didn't want you to have to do it. As much as you wanted to, you would've regretted it. I would've, too, if you hadn't taken the choice from me with my parents."

"You knew?"

"I suspected and Paulo confirmed it. I think my story triggered something in you about Kyle and what your father did. You just didn't realize you were working off a memory," Law explained. "It's over, baby. This is over and the rest of it's just beginning."

The men put their heads together, foreheads touching, for a long moment in the frigid cold.

"I'm your past—he's your future," Styx told him.

"My past is part of my future—always will be, if I have anything to say about it. And I damn well have everything to say about it."

"Stubborn."

"You like me that way. Always have," he murmured, and Styx couldn't object.

"Always, Law," Styx agreed. "But you've got to go back to the cabin to make sure it's really over—that no one else is coming for any of us."

"You're coming?"

"No—you and Paulo. My director wants a report. I have to, Law."

Law didn't say anything at first and then finally told Styx, "You do what you need to. But remember, we need you."

"I'll remember," Styx told him before he pulled away reluctantly, watched Law and Tanner and Damon get hustled into a waiting SUV.

Law watched Styx standing on the corner from the window of the moving car until Styx was out of sight…and even then, he refused to turn back around.

19

Law and Paulo remained at the cabin with Damon for a week, while Tanner had been ushered right back into service, before the CIA cleared them to go home.

Paulo was told his family had been allowed to do so as well, but he told Law he didn't want to make contact with them, and Law hadn't pushed him.

Damon and Tanner had already cleaned up Law's place for him and Paulo's too, but they only stopped at Paulo's apartment so he could grab a few necessities. And then they were in Law's truck, making the short drive to his apartment, where the men dropped their bags by the door.

"Place looks great—you'll have to give me the tour," Paulo said.

"We'll move you out of your place and into here over the next few weeks," Law told him.

"Ah, we're in the I'll-make-all-the-decisions-for-you phase, are we?"

Law locked an arm around his waist and dragged him close. "Problem with that?"

"Even if I did, all you have to do is throw me on the bed and I'll forget my own name."

Law raised his brows. "Let's try that theory out."

He picked up Paulo and put him over his shoulder, walked him through the apartment until he reached the king-sized bed.

Law did throw him down, stripped him, climbed him in what seemed like seconds, then let the man catch his breath.

"Fuck, you're good at that," Paulo said as Law took his own shirt off and started to take down his jeans.

Paulo reached up to stroke Law's cheek. Paulo still bore the bruises from what had happened—Law knew he'd always bear scars…but it would heal underneath.

Scars made the skin tougher anyway.

"Lots of room in this bed."

"You're thinking about him too?"

"Thinking. Worrying." Law looked at him. "Same as we worried about you."

"Never going to let me live that down, are you?"

"Never," Law agreed, but he was smiling a little. "You know, Greg said that the people who need us the most are drawn to us, no matter how we try to outrun them. They find us and eventually they heal us, no matter how resistant we are."

"And you were resistant to anything, more than I ever was," Paulo reminded him, and Law swore he could almost hear Styx's laugh, deep and easy in its agreement.

There was so much to discover—he wanted to find out something new every damned day. "You and Styx both like it that way. You want to be the ones who break me out of the stubbornness."

"Hallelujah, he finally gets it," Paulo said with a smile. "He'll come back."

"And if he doesn't, am I enough?"

"I could ask you the same question."

Law smiled. "You always were. This was never about needing more."

"I know." Paulo tugged on his arm. "Come on, show me that anyway."

Law did, kissed his way down Paulo's back, licking the pattern of the tats as he went, while Paulo remained on his hands and knees, waiting.

"You still need…to get your tat," Paulo breathed.

When Law's hand finally circled his dick, Paulo groaned and Law let the hard column rest in his palm, wanting to drive the younger man crazy. "I will. How about the three of us go together?"

Paulo nodded, his face flushed. "I like. Now fuck me, old man."

"You're in so much goddamned trouble," Law muttered, and then proceeded to show Paulo just how much for the next several hours.

Styx knew that the two men had moved into Law's apartment, the top floor of the building so they had more space. Paulo opened the PI business with Law, and they waited for Styx to run himself out, not doing more than calling him to tell him they missed him, texting him to keep safe. All of it done with a light enough touch to where he didn't feel cornered.

He finished up some loose ends with the CIA. Had several long talks with Tomcat and, in the end, made up his own mind. A decision he could live with.

There were no more memories, maybe mercifully so. Styx really hadn't wanted to know more—bad enough that he had the bloodlines of that assassin inside of him.

Don't go there, Styx.

Styx, that's who he was…reborn on that park bench at sixteen, reborn because of Greg and loved by two men he loved and respected.

What the hell else could he ask for? Some people never got second chances. Some never even got a first.

It took six months, but one night, he turned the key Law had sent him in the lock and walked in as Law and Paulo watched.

He'd thought they'd be pissed. Expected it, because he'd always been a realist. But there was more relief than anything in Paulo's and Law's eyes.

"Sorry. Didn't mean to make you worry."

"You can make it up to us," Law told him.

The men embraced him, tugged him into the bedroom where they literally stripped and then cuffed him to the bed. Styx didn't bother to fight the bonds, just lay back and enjoyed the men watching him like he was their goddamned main course.

They didn't bother to ask questions—they'd all waited too long for this moment. Hell, Styx had been dreaming about it, and so when both men came forward to each capture a nipple in their teeth and tug, he bucked and groaned. Called out both *Law* and *Paulo* in rapid succession and watched as the men took their time kissing their way down his chest toward his cock.

"If you two make me wait much longer…" he finally growled, and Law laughed and looked at Paulo.

"Maybe we should take some pity on him," he said, and Paulo nodded and licked around the piercing and yeah, that was what he needed. He watched as Law guided Paulo's head up and down, slicking his cock up. Law's hand circled Paulo's cock and Paulo moaned, the vibrations catching Styx's cock and nearly making him lose control.

But that was what all this was about, in the end. Surrendering to what he needed. What he'd always wanted. With Paulo, that was an unexpected and very much needed surprise. He'd somehow become the glue that kept Law and

Styx from tearing each other apart and fucking things up again.

It had taken him a long time to feel lucky. But he was there now.

Law was watching him carefully, spoke when Styx's eyes met his. "I hope you have the time and the energy for both of us tonight."

"Now you're calling…me…old?" Styx managed as Paulo deep-throated him. "You fucker. You're…going…over my knee."

"Yeah, I was kind of hoping that," Law confessed, and Paulo laughed around Styx's cock. "How long do we have you for?" Law asked, and Paulo paused, took his mouth away to wait for the answer.

"As long as you want me," Styx said.

"That's simple—forever, then," Law said, and Paulo echoed, "Forever."

He'd finally come home, and he had the memories to prove it.

NEWSLETTER

Sign up for the newsletter of SE Jakes and her alter-ego Stephanie Tyler!

Be among the first to learn not only about new and upcoming books but also appearances and signings as well as special promotions and giveaways!

http://stephanietyler.com/newsletter/

NOW AVAILABLE:

BOUND BY HONOR
MEN OF HONOR

TURN THE PAGE TO READ MORE...

MEN OF HONOR, BOOK 1

A promise forces two men to bare themselves...
completely.

One year ago on a mission gone wrong, Tanner James failed to save the life of Jesse, his Army Ranger teammate. Before dying in that South American jungle, Jesse extracted a promise that won't let Tanner rest until it's fulfilled—no matter what it costs him.

Damon Price loved Jesse, but problems in their relationship had come to a head right before Jesse left on his final mission. Now a reluctant Dom and a man still in mourning, he's not happy when Tanner appears at his BDSM club. And even less happy with Jesse's last request—that Tanner sub for him for one night.

After a rough start, Damon realizes that the tough soldier, despite his protests, aches for someone to take control. And Tanner senses a hesitance, an insecurity in Damon that makes him wonder if he's simply a placeholder for Jesse, or if their tentative connection could grow into something more.

For Jesse's sake, they agree to try one weekend together. Then duty calls, and a series of attacks that have been happening near the club hits too close to home, making both men wonder if giving their hearts is a maneuver fraught with too much risk...

Warning: Contains rough language, rougher sex and
warriors who fall hard for each other.

Tanner James had been to hell and back more times than he could count over the course of his twenty-six years and was always pretty sure he'd live to make the trip again. But this time, even as adrenaline raced through his body and every muscle tensed for battle, hell beckoned with a one-way ticket and without a goddamned firefight in sight.

No, that would've been easier, *much* easier than this slow crawl to the door of Crave—a BDSM club with the reputation of being both accessible and safe—the week before Christmas.

He looked up at the dark sign with white lettering at the entrance and thought about turning back and going home.

If he hadn't promised Jesse that he'd do this, that he'd look up Jesse's former boyfriend, he'd be home right now, having just returned from a month-long mission, not about to offer himself up like some bondage sacrifice.

This wasn't his scene. Not really. He was all about rough sex, was bisexual with a definite preference to men for as long as he could remember, used to having to *don't ask, don't tell*, thanks to his military career—but this? Having to go in and greet the owner with a message from his dead lover? Well, that was fucking weird and could get him thrown out on his ass.

Jesus Christ, this was going to suck.

The man checking patrons who entered was dressed in bright, loud colors. Tight black leather pants. Guyliner. And he flirted in an over-the-top manner with anyone he deemed hot enough.

Tanner knew he'd be the subject of the man's flirtation. Although he'd shrugged it off his entire life, the looks and stares and come-ons he'd been on the receiving end of forever told him he was handsome.

He was more interested in being the best Army Ranger he could, spent most days knee-deep in jungle crap with paint on his face and men who only cared that he could shoot an M-14 with dizzying accuracy.

"Hey."

"Hello, gorgeous. Please tell me you're alone." The man peeked behind Tanner, saw no one and clapped his hands. "Alone. There is a God."

"I'm looking for Damon Price."

"I'll bet you are," the man said with a shake of his head. "Shame, really, that they all want what they can't have."

"I just need to talk to him."

The man erupted into peals of girlish laughter and Tanner rolled his eyes. He'd never been into queens and this was why. If he was going to fuck a man, he was going to fuck a man. "Tell him I've got a message from Jesse."

The man stopped, nearly choked, but before he could answer, he was elbowed out of the way by a much taller blond man—ruggedly handsome although unsmiling, and Tanner wondered if he was face to face with Damon himself.

But rather than introduce himself, he asked, "What did you say about Jesse?"

"You heard me," Tanner bit out.

The man nodded slowly. "I heard you. I just don't know how Damon's going to feel about this." He paused. "Are you sure you want to go there?"

Tanner reacted before he could stop himself. "Why the *fuck* would you care where I want to go?"

The man raised a brow and held up a finger, indicating for Tanner to wait a minute, before disappearing down a back hallway.

Last chance to head for the hills. And despite the ease with which he could do so, Tanner remained rooted in place.

He couldn't see very far into the club at all from where he stood—it was designed purposely to let the incoming patrons hear the familiar sounds of sex occasionally rising over the music. The smell of sex was also unmistakable, partially hidden and mixed with whiskey and smoke. It was meant to beckon, to lead men astray…and Tanner didn't bother to hide his hard-on.

A few minutes later, Tanner was being led by the blond man who introduced himself as LC back to a private office with a big *Do Not Disturb* sign on the door.

No doubt, *this* counted as disturbing Damon, but it had been eating away at Tanner for a year now. He had to rid himself of this burden, do what Jesse asked and then go home and pretend none of it ever happened.

Before going in, he glanced at his watch. Just after midnight. Exactly the way Jesse had wanted it.

A hard growl of a voice called, "Come in."

LC stared at him, and Tanner, in turn, stared at the floor for a long moment. And then he opened the door and realized he'd been anything but prepared for Damon Price. Tanner was big and broad and strong, stood six foot three and turned heads wherever he went. But Damon—he was well over six foot five, with jet black hair and chiseled features. He stood, hands at his sides in a deceptively casual stance, dressed in full black leather and looking like a fucking badass.

Tanner nearly hyperventilated, because Jesse hadn't mentioned this part.

"He's my boyfriend and he owns a club," was all Jesse said. *"He's strong—reminds me of you. He's a Dom."*

"I'm not a Dom."

"No. But you could probably use one. It would be the only kind of man who could handle you."

Jesse had closed his eyes then before Tanner could tell him he had no interest in being anyone's bottom boy. Because Jesse had been talking to him about boyfriends and Doms when he'd been dying, slowly and painfully in the middle of a jungle in South America where he and his Ranger team had been on a mission, and Tanner had been fucking helpless to stop it.

Fuck.

He shoved his hands in his pockets so Damon wouldn't see the fists he couldn't uncurl and hoped the pain didn't show in his eyes.

This was supposed to bring closure—to both Damon and Tanner. There was no way to break a promise to a dead man.

Damon studied him for a few minutes. Tanner wasn't the type to squirm and he wasn't about to start now. Finally, the man said, "I hear you have a message from Jesse. And I swear to Christ, if you're fucking with me, I'll put your head through the wall."

Tanner snorted in spite of himself. "Okay, sure. I'd like to see you try."

Damon pushed away from the desk and stood toe-to-toe with him. "Talk."

Talk. Yeah, like it was that easy. "Jesse told me to come here—to ask for you. To tell you that…" Fuck. He shifted, aware that the proximity of Damon was freaking him out. If he hadn't been Jesse's, Tanner might've made a move without a second thought.

As if he knew what he was thinking, Damon arched an eyebrow at him, his lip curled into a half sneer.

Fuck it all. "I'm supposed to tell you to have a session with me. Jesse wanted it that way." "A session?" Damon repeated.

"Yeah. I'm supposed to let you Dom me. It was Jesse's dying wish."

Damon paled, took a step back from Tanner, and then another. "Is this a sick joke?"

"Do I look like I'm joking?"

"You little fuck." Damon had Tanner's shirt bunched in his fists, was slamming him against the office wall hard. "You sick bastard. You think you can ingratiate yourself to me by using Jesse?"

Tanner ground his teeth together hard and tamped back his anger. He'd known Damon wouldn't take this well. If Tanner had been in the same position, he doubted he would either. "He asked me to wait a year before I came here. He died after midnight."

"How do you know that?" Damon demanded. "Even I don't know that."

No, he wouldn't. The mission was deemed classified— and Jesse's time of death a closely guarded secret. "I was with him when he died."

Damon let out a long, hissing breath and let go of Tanner's shirt.

"I'm sorry—I didn't know how else to tell you. Jesse made me promise—"

"Stop saying his name," Damon growled hoarsely.

"He made me promise I'd wait the year. Said you wouldn't be ready before that. That you'd need to be dragged back into the land of the living, kicking and screaming. He said to tell you…to use the skull- and-crossbones collar with the broken latch." He spoke fast, stopped to catch his breath at the end. Gauged Damon's reaction.

The man hadn't moved a muscle during Tanner's speech. Simply stared, and Tanner tensed more, wondering if he was going to have to fight tonight.

Fighting and fucking were definitely two of his favorite things to do, sometimes all in the same night—or hour—or hell, the same time, but he had a feeling that he'd be pushing his luck taking on this guy.

He was in way over his head. And he couldn't remember the last time—if ever—he'd felt that way.

Damon's features relaxed slightly. He sat back on the top of the desk, folded his arms and stared Tanner up and down. A hard, assessing stare that was enough to make Tanner hard with desire and anticipation.

He wasn't sure why the sudden thought of Damon taking him got him hot, but that was short-lived, because he saw the tension in Damon's stance, the pain in his eyes. Tanner wanted to apologize, but he wasn't sure what for. Wanted to tell Damon that he was scared to fucking death that the

Domming would actually happen—and also scared that it wouldn't.

He was so fucked up he could barely see straight.

Damon finally spoke. "I wouldn't touch you. You're not man enough to handle me."

Jesse's words echoed in Tanner's ear. *It would be the only kind of man who could handle you.*

Tanner hadn't been able to handle a relationship—or being touched, really, since what happened to Jesse last year. And so he nodded and he said, "You're right about that. This was a mistake."

The failure hanging on him heavily, he pushed out the door, went through the club and headed for the parking lot.

Jesse.

Damon had mourned over that man, cried over him, beat his fists against the wall, up until three months earlier. Things had eased, but he still wore the cloak of grief that sometimes threatened to choke him.

Now was one of those times. He'd waited until the gorgeous man left his office before he fell apart and tried his best not to hyperventilate.

Use the skull-and-crossbones collar with the broken latch.

The boy who'd just left his office would have no way of knowing that—wouldn't have known that Damon kept that collar in his loft, had fixed the latch right after Jesse died because it was one of the only things he could do.

Damon wouldn't be able to use the damned collar on this boy—Jesse knew that collaring meant something—that it didn't happen on a first night together.

You don't even know the boy's name.

He shuddered involuntarily that he'd thought of him as *the boy*. Because that's what he'd called Jesse—and only Jesse.

Jesse had been the first to ever thaw what Damon had considered a heart of ice. First, and the *only*.

But something tugged at his gut.

He could've been lying. This could be part of an elaborate scam.

The only thing was, the man had definitely been military. A Ranger, like Jesse, or so he said. Damon didn't doubt it, had a nose for those things, having been in special forces himself what seemed like a lifetime ago. And the timing was exactly right. Jesse had died a year ago, nearly to the hour, although he'd lied to the boy about not having that information.

Fuck.

He called through the open office door, "LC, grab that guy who just left."

"I'm not your bitch," LC drawled, and no, LC was no one's bitch…not since Styx left. "And he's already in the lot."

"Dammit."

LC held his gaze for a second and then called to one of the bodyguards. "Renn—grab the guy in the brown leather jacket who just left. And bring a few guys—he won't come willingly."

LC didn't say anything more, didn't have to, and just headed to the front of the club to supervise. And Damon waited in his office, trying not to pace. Trying not to picture what the boy would look like, bound and spread for him.

Trying to pretend he wasn't hard at the thought of it.

He shifted but could do nothing to hide the erection in the pants he wore, and when LC barged back into the office, it was the first thing he noticed.

Thankfully, he didn't comment on it, just said, "They've got him and he's not happy."

"Makes two of us."

"Did he really know Jesse?"

Damon nodded. "He says that Jesse sent him here—wanted him to have a session with me."

LC's eyes widened, but wisely his mouth remained closed. He was part owner of Crave, working mainly behind the scenes. He was also Damon's best friend—the only person Damon confided everything in. The only one he trusted enough to let him run the business in those months after Jesse died, when Damon couldn't get out of bed most days. LC had finally gotten him up and functioning.

Just then, the boy was dragged back in by three men—he was pissed for sure, but not fighting as hard as he could.

Damon knew that, and whether it was grief or curiosity or both, he couldn't tell yet.

"Let him go," Damon commanded, and the men dropped him and left the room with LC, the office door shutting behind them as the boy stumbled forward until Damon caught him, held him hard by the biceps and stared at him again.

He was handsome as hell—all-American-looking, a blond haired, blue-eyed devil, even with his lips twisted into an angry grimace.

"What the fuck do you think you're doing?" The boy jerked out of his grasp and yes, he was strong. Damon had suspected as much. Earlier, when Damon had him by the shirt, backed against the wall, he hadn't flinched. It was the calm of a man who knew how to fight—who knew how to kill.

"What's your name?"

A jut of a chin, a glint of wild eyes and he ground out, "Tanner."

"Why did you come here?"

"Because I made a promise to Jesse when he was dying. I don't break promises like that."

"And you're willing to follow through on what he wanted."

Tanner pressed his lips together—he wanted to say no, that much Damon knew. For some reason, this handsome, strong, brave man wanted nothing to do with being

Dommed, and it didn't appear to be for the usual reasons.

No, he wasn't uncomfortable, either in this club or with Damon and his leathers. But something was most definitely wrong with him.

"I'll do what Jesse wanted, yes."

"But you don't think you're man enough."

He waited for Tanner to snap an answer back, but none came. Instead, he shrugged.

"Well then, there's no time like the present. But no collar." He motioned for Tanner to follow him, out the door of the office, down a small hallway and into a room marked Room Four.

Once inside, Damon pressed a few buttons to bring the lights up and to remove the shading from the plate-glass divider that separated the room from the rest of the club.

As soon as he did so, the bar began to cheer. Damon activated the two-way speakers as well, so the sounds went from muffled to completely clear.

Tanner's eyes widened. "We're doing this here—where everyone can see?"

"Yes. That's what Jesse would've wanted."

Tanner couldn't have known that was the furthest thing from the truth—that Jesse understood the value of privacy at the start of a D/s relationship.

That Jesse would hate him for this.

Well, Damon hated Jesse for dying and leaving him. For refusing to quit the military and let Damon take care of him for the rest of his life.

For recognizing that Damon had been slowly dying inside during the last year of their relationship and continuing to satisfy his own needs instead.

Tanner swallowed hard and then he nodded.

Yes, let's see if this man is for real.

NOW AVAILABLE:

TIES THAT BIND

MEN OF HONOR

TURN THE PAGE FOR A SNEAK PEEK...

MEN OF HONOR, BOOK 3

Can two men let go of the past in order to find their future together?

When helo pilot Glen Rhodes flies Navy SEALS into the most dangerous places on earth, he has nerves of steel. Since his trusted Dom's death three years ago, though, the thought of submitting makes him panic.

Determined to move on and long past ready to release the adrenaline rush from his job, Glen returns to home ground—and to the bar he hasn't had the heart to enter for three long years. There, he meets a man who seems to fit naturally into the void.

Derek Mann has suffered his own losses, and he isn't looking for permanent. Easy conquests don't interest him, either. One look at Glen's proud military bearing and sad eyes tells him that he has a challenge on his hands. And that winning Glen's trust will unleash something wild and beautiful.

The plan is to tread lightly. But from the first touch of skin on skin, there's no holding back...except when it comes to their deepest emotions. A Christmas Eve crisis pushes them both to their limits, leaving them no choice but to let go of the past...or let it pull them apart.

Warning: Contains rough language, rougher sex and warriors who fall hard for one another.

1

Glen Rhodes remembered the first time he'd snuck into the leather bar. He'd been seventeen with a good fake ID, and he'd fought with the first man he'd encountered. Hadn't expected to be grabbed and treated like he was there for the taking.

Hadn't understood he'd been in way over his head. If it hadn't been for John…

John was big and broad, a bear in every sense of the word, but Glen hadn't been looking for a bear, just a man to help him deal with his submissive needs.

It had been confusing as hell, and John had helped him make sense out of his wants. Until then, Glen's life consisted of competitive swimming and little else, to the point where he'd started to feel closed in. Constricted.

The panic attacks that began that year had made everything worse. He'd talked to coaches and shrinks, but nothing they recommended helped defuse the frustration. The road to the Olympics was a long one, filled with days and nights of constant practice. Physical stamina was a must, but mental toughness was a necessity—the other half of the puzzle.

It wasn't until he stumbled on BDSM porn one night that he realized what he might be missing. It turned him on like nothing else had.

How to go about getting it was a different story. Fantasy took him only so far, and even though he wasn't hiding his sexuality, there weren't any seventeen- year-old boys he knew who were willing—or able—to tie him up the way he needed.

John gave him that outlet.

John took him home, tied him to the headboard and let him come. And then he'd left him tied for hours and took Glen in ways he'd only seen or read about.

"Virgin," John had murmured, and it hadn't been a problem for him at all.

From that point on, John gave him what he needed without Glen having to do much more than show up. Other types of submission were not for him—he liked spankings but not whips or punishments—he'd urged John to try both with him a few times but it ended in disaster because Glen simply couldn't get off.

Rope bondage or cuffs or spreader bars—Jesus, sometimes just seeing a ball of twine got him hard. And the submission with John focused Glen on his swimming, to the point where he had an amazing Olympic career in front of him if things continued along that vein.

They hadn't. And while he and John were never exclusive, John had always been there for him. His touchstone. He'd assumed, in that naïve way you had when you were young that you and everyone around you would live forever.

Now, a little over ten years later, the bar looked the same. He'd been back here a few times since John's death five years ago, trying a new Dom less than a year after John died.

Too soon. Wrong Dom. Since then, nothing had seemed right, and he just kept one foot in front of the other, did his job and fucked as many men as he could.

Since then, he hadn't let anyone else in—literally, figuratively—and he wasn't sure why he'd turned the car in this direction tonight, why he stood outside, listening to the music and the laughter. It wasn't even Thanksgiving yet, and the lights blinked along the windows, wreath hung on the door… Glen wouldn't be able to escape the time of year.

Christmas always hit Glen hard. John had died in the weeks prior, and although some said Glen should've moved on by now, he hadn't been able to.

But lately, the numbness had been replaced by a deep ache he couldn't fill, no matter how often he fucked random guys.

It was time to allow himself to be tied up again. Whether or not he would find the right Dom remained to be seen. But he'd start at the club he'd met John in, because they knew him. They'd protect him, although he felt stupid for even thinking he'd need that.

You're vulnerable—you need it, his friend Clint, aka Tomcat, had told him the week before. He'd met Clint years earlier, through John's work. John had been with the CIA, although Glen doubted anyone in the Dom/sub world who knew the man would know that. And although Glen rarely saw Clint, they spoke often, with Clint checking up on him at least every couple of months.

And so, because of Clint's words, Glen swallowed his pride and went toward the comfort of the old club, where there were rules and regulations, and not everyone who said they were a Dom was allowed through the door.

He'd promised he wouldn't do anything dumb but damn, he wanted to be fucked stupid—and soon.

A shiver brushed the back of Derek's neck seconds before he spotted the blond walk through the door.

The boy was beautiful—handsome, maybe mid-to-late twenties. The tattoos that ran up and down his arms were a promise of many more under the black wife-beater that he revealed when the black leather jacket slipped off.

He turned to the older Dom, James, sitting next to him at the bar. "Who's that?"

"That's Glen," James said with a half-smile. He'd been watching the boy as well. "I didn't think we'd ever see him here again."

Derek's gut tugged—usually that meant the boy was a pain in the ass or not a good sub at all. But typically, this bar wouldn't allow someone like that inside. "Why not?"

James pointed to the wall and Derek turned his head toward the picture of John.

"He was John's?" John was a legend at this place—part-owner, friend to all. A Dom who taught others what the term really meant. He'd also been retired CIA, although Derek was only privy to that because of his own time in the military.

"For five years, until John died. After that…" James shook his head. "He's never taken another Dom?"

"He tried. But it didn't work. John was a hard memory to live up to." "Maybe he tried someplace else?"

"No way—this is Glen's home. He knows that. John wouldn't have wanted him to go someplace he wasn't known to sub. He's been fucking around in other bars, literally, but that's about it." James looked at Derek. "If he's back here, that means he's looking."

"Any advice?" Because Derek was chomping at the bit to approach him. The shiver touched his neck again and he rubbed the skin there and wondered why this boy hit him so hard.

James fixed him with a hard gaze. "He's not easy. Never was, never will be. He doesn't want the traditional relationship. But if he respects you, the submission you get…"

James didn't finish but Derek knew—could tell by the strut the boy had, even with the sadness in his eyes—that Glen submitting would be a wild and beautiful thing. He'd had that once, a long time ago, and some said he'd been purposely picking the wrong boys since.

They were probably right.

A widowed Dom and a widowed sub typically didn't mix well—both had expectations that were impossible to meet. But he was being tugged in Glen's direction by something, and he glanced at the picture of John and back to Glen.

He watched the other men come up to the boy, hug him, welcome him as he drank his beer slowly. Glen looked overwhelmed after about fifteen minutes, was having trouble making eye contact with people, had his hands stuffed in his pockets, and Derek could see they were fisted. He couldn't think of a better time to make his introduction.

He came up behind the boy and put a hand on the back of his neck, his palm tingling with the contact of the warm skin. Glen stilled immediately and Derek murmured, "Come on—you're about to lose it."

Glen didn't fight, turned and walked next to Derek, not meeting his eyes, walking with his head down. Derek kept up the light rub on his hot skin until they moved to a more private area, ignoring the whispers that started immediately.

"Face the wall," Derek told him.

"I don't do that punishment shit," Glen growled, tried to

break away but Derek held him in place, inhaling the boy's scent—beach and cinnamon and that pure scent of a man aroused.

"It's not a punishment. You're on sensory overload, headed to a panic attack.

Now stay. Breathe."

Glen gave a short nod, a flash of appreciation in his dark blue eyes, and did just that. Hung his head, stuffed his hands in his pockets again, and the men remained silent for a few minutes until Glen's breathing became slow and steady. Derek studied his profile—his bearing was military, straight and sure, even with his head down with the kind of perfect posture of a sub. Derek had an urge to kiss him, but that would only end in disaster at the moment.

"Thanks," Glen said finally, lifted his head and looked Derek in the eye. Half challenge, but there was also something else there…uncertainty. Lust, too.

It was enough. "I'm Derek Mann. Come sit. Have a drink."

Glen nodded, sat next to Derek on the couch but asked for a soda when the waiter came to take their order. The waiter obviously recognized Glen, nodded at him, and Glen nodded back and drank half the Coke on his first pull. "I guess you know who I am."

"I know who your Dom was," Derek said. "That's not the same thing at all."

Glen frowned a little, as if he'd never considered that.

"You're the only one who had the balls to approach me like that." That obviously sat well with Glen— with Derek too.

"Are you here to play?"

Glen stared at him, the dark blue eyes holding more pain than should be allowed for a young man. "I'm here to get fucked," he said bluntly. "After that…"

Derek let the corner of his mouth tug up. Glen would be a challenge, as promised. Broken wasn't a word in his vocabulary. "You're military."

"Navy pilot." "Before that?"

"I was headed to the Olympics. Swimming." "What happened?"

The challenge was back in his eyes. "John died and I gave up on everything. I figured if I could do something dangerous, I'd die sooner and then not break my promise to John."

"Which was?" Derek had no right to ask, but he did.

Glen looked right into his eyes, his answer unapologetic. "Not to kill myself after he died."

Why he told the dark-haired Dom that partial lie—since he'd already been in the military when John died—Glen wasn't sure.

Bullshit you're not sure—you want to scare him away.

But the Dom—with the dark brown eyes and chiseled

cheekbones and lips that made Glen lick his involuntarily—didn't seem shocked. Sad, maybe, but without the typical pity shit, which Glen had no use for.

Derek was big—broad, muscular—wore his leathers well. His chest and face were smooth—the total opposite of John in every way and it still made Glen hot.

Glen wasn't small but next to this guy…

A flash of fantasy—of being pinned under the Dom, helpless. Being filled until he didn't think he could take any more. Surrendering.

Damn, it had been so long for him. Fucking guys wasn't giving him anything close to what he needed, and it had taken a trip in here and Derek's touch to make him admit it to himself.

He swore he heard John whispering to him, but he couldn't make out the words.

John. And that made him think of Mark and how bad that scene was, even though the man was as handsome as Derek.

"This was a mistake." He made a move to stand, but Derek held him firmly by the wrist, looked him in the eye and Glen swore the man was hypnotizing him somehow.

"You're looking for a fuck. I'm willing to give you what you need—where's the mistake in that?" Derek asked calmly. "That's not rhetorical, by the way. I expect an answer."

"I can't…not here." He couldn't go into the back rooms, with all the memories. Everything was welling up and his breath was coming fast again and the smells of beer and sex and cologne were stifling him.

"Your place." Derek stood and Glen found himself doing so automatically as well, mainly because Derek still held his wrist. He let go so Glen could put his jacket on and then Derek's hand went on the back of his neck again, leading him through the bar and into the parking lot. "Don't make eye contact with anyone."

Glen didn't argue—Derek was telling him for his own good. And once he hit the uncrowded space, he took a big lungful of air and glanced toward Derek.

The man hadn't taken his eyes off him. Glen felt…taken care of. Owned. His body missed that feeling.

So much so, he was willing to throw himself at the first guy who showed him attention.

But that wasn't really true.

Derek's voice broke through his reverie. "Did you drive?" Glen pointed to the old Porsche.

"Beautiful baby," Derek whispered as he steered them in its direction, and Glen had the feeling the man wasn't talking only about the car. "Drive me in it."

An order…a request, and it really didn't matter. Glen would take him home. The men in the club wouldn't have let him leave with Derek if the man hadn't been sane, safe, consensual, no matter if Glen met their eyes or not.

Derek stretched his legs as far as he could in the low machine—the seats were all the way back—and the Dom leaned back and closed his eyes as Glen rumbled out of the lot and headed to the highway.

His townhouse was half an hour from the club—he lived close to the base but not on it, because he needed that cushion of privacy, since *don't ask, don't tell* was still very much a reality, repeal or not. Besides, his private life had never been anyone's business. The Navy got its time and Glen got his, and that was the end of it.

He looked over quickly at Derek, whose eyes were still closed, his big body relaxed, but his cock definitely hard. Glen's own had been that way since Derek touched him. He could still feel the man's hand on his neck even though he'd let go fifteen minutes ago.

How was this man getting home from his place? Where did he even live?

Glen found himself driving more carefully than normal, as if wanting to keep Derek from being jostled. He finally pulled into his driveway and then the garage, letting the door close behind him.

Derek got out immediately, and Glen found the man opening the driver's- side door and helping him out. And Glen fucking blushed at that.

Derek most definitely noticed, gave a little twist of a grin, and Glen felt himself blush harder as he got out of the car and let Derek lead him toward his own house.

"It's okay," Derek murmured and somehow, with the Dom saying that, it was. At least for the moment. What happened once the door opened and Glen let him in, he wasn't sure at all.

ALSO BY SE JAKES

Men of Honor Series
BOUND BY HONOR
BOUND BY LAW
TIES THAT BIND
BOUND BY DANGER
BOUND FOR KEEPS
BOUND TO BREAK

Phoenix, Inc. Series
NO BOUNDARIES

Inked Series
HOLD THE LINE
THIRDS

EE LTD. Universe
FREE FALLING

Hell or High Water Series
CATCH A GHOST
LONG TIME GONE
DAYLIGHT AGAIN
NOT FADE AWAY
IF I EVER *(forthcoming)*

Dirty Deeds Series
DIRTY DEEDS

Havoc MC Series
RUNNING WILD

Bluewater Bay (multi-author series)
NO EASY WAY (novella) in the *LIGHTS, CAMERA,
ACTION* Anthology

WRITING AS
STEPHANIE TYLER

Shelter Series
SHELTER ME
PIECES OF ME (coming Fall 2016)

Mirror Series
MIRROR ME
RULE OF THIRDS
WALK IN MY SHADOW
DOUBLE BLIND (coming 2017)

Skulls Creek MC Series
VIPERS RUN
VIPERS RULE

Section 8 Series
SURRENDER
UNBREAKABLE
FRAGMENTED

WRITING AS SYDNEY CROFT

ACRO Series
RIDING THE STORM
UNLEASHING THE STORM
SEDUCED BY THE STORM
TAMING THE FIRE
TEMPTING THE FIRE
TAKEN BY FIRE
THREE THE HARD WAy (novella)

Hot Nights, Dark Desires Anthology
SHADOW PLAY (novella)

ABOUT THE AUTHOR

SE JAKES is the pen name for *New York Times* bestselling author Stephanie Tyler, and half the co-writing team of Sydney Croft. First published in 2011, SE Jakes has quickly risen to be a bestselling author in the LGBT romance genre, as well as a fan favorite. Her books are frequently highlighted in *USA Today* and have been reviewed by *Library Journal* and *RT Books Magazine*. She's been nominated by several sites for Favorite M/M author and has finaled in the Goodreads M/M Romance Readers Choice Awards in 7 categories. She's a hybrid author who writes for Riptide Publishing and Samhain Publishing, and she indie publishes as well.

STEPHANIE TYLER is the *New York Times* bestselling author of romance novels spanning multiple genres, including Romantic Suspense, New Adult, Paranormal Romance and Contemporary Romance. She's a hybrid author who writes for multiple publishers, including Random House, NAL/Penguin, Harlequin, Carina Press, Mammoth Books, Belle Books and Samhain Publishing, as well as Riptide (as SE Jakes) and indie publishing. Her books have been translated into half a dozen languages, nominated for an RT Readers' Choice Award and garnered top picks from *RT Book Magazine* as well as starred reviews from *Publishers Weekly*. She's a frequent workshop presenter and has contributed stories for anthologies for charities, including **SEAL of My Dreams**, which has raised over 150K for the Veterans Medical Association.

SYDNEY CROFT is the alter ego of Stephanie Tyler and Larissa Ione, two *New York Times* bestselling authors who blend their very different writing interests into adventurous tales of erotic paranormal fiction. Together, they developed a world where people with extraordinary abilities, like the power to control storms, could live and work with others like them. The series has been described as "Erotica meets the X-Men," and is unique in its own "erotic superhero romance" niche. Larissa and Stephanie live in different states and communicate almost entirely through email, though they often get together for conferences and book signings.